If the B

MW00473054

by

Sara Bourgeois

can buy as soon as I have some money to buy one."

Not one to tempt fate, though at the time I didn't really believe in it, I jumped into the car and checked my side mirror for oncoming traffic. There was none, so I pulled out onto the dusty country highway as smoothly as possible.

A few minutes later, Coventry loomed on the horizon. One thing I couldn't get over about the Midwest was how flat everything was. I could see for miles in every direction as long as I wasn't surrounded by corn fields. Which I frequently was...

As the car rolled into Coventry, I still wasn't sure what to expect. I'd been in my fair share of small towns, and each of them held their own particular quirks and comforts. But my grandmother, Eunice Tuttlesmith-Bridger, had spoken of Coventry with such loathing. On the other hand, my beloved great-aunt, "Mad" Maude Tuttlesmith, had loved Coventry. She'd spoken highly of the town all the way to her death.

4

I ultimately decided that it didn't matter. Coventry was a short layover in my life. It wasn't as if I planned on spending much time there, so it didn't matter how I felt about the town. I could adapt to anything for a few weeks or months. I had already had to adapt to the end of my marriage and the fact that I was childless. Whatever secrets and scandals Coventry held, I could acclimate.

As I drove through town, I became keenly aware that everyone was staring at me. People would turn completely around from what they were doing to gape at me openly. After I quickly checked my hair and face for smudges or giant boogers, I concluded that my mere presence had been judged strange enough to warrant the glares.

I'd passed through small towns before, but I had never drawn that much attention. "Must be the U-Haul," I said to myself. One thing was evident. Living there was going to be far different than life in the city. In the city everyone tried hard to pretend not to notice anyone else. They certainly didn't all turn around and watch people they'd never met the way the citizens of Coventry did. I felt like a criminal, but I knew I hadn't done anything wrong.

Not wanting to be inspected any longer, I checked the directions I'd written out. I'd been advised my GPS would be useless in Coventry because it was on some sort of magnetic anomaly or something, and then sped up.

My first impression of Hangman's House was underwhelming at best. As I parked the car in the narrow gravel driveway, I could only hope that the inside was in better shape. The outside was a decaying old Victorian with at least two stories. There was possibly a third, or it could have been an attic space with windows. The paint was peeling, and some of the windows were boarded over. I hoped that was to protect them from the elements and not because they were broken.

I got out of the car and retrieved my purse from the passenger side. After digging out the keys, I took a deep breath and crossed the patchy lawn to the weathered front steps.

The first step was the scariest. The worn, gray boards looked as though they might not hold my weight. I winced at the groan the riser made when I stepped up and it bent slightly, but the old wood held.

"I'm going to have to get this fixed or someone is going to hurt themselves and sue me," I said to no one in particular.

The rest of the steps were equally creaky as were the wood planks of the front porch. I figured that at the very least, it would be hard for someone to sneak up on me. Not that there was any reason for me to believe that someone would want to sneak up on me.

I put the key in the deadbolt on the front door and turned it slowly. The door opened with a loud creak, and I stepped through gingerly. There was no reason for me to expect that something might jump out at me, but the fear lingered there in the back of my mind. I'd spent too many nights watching horror movies alone in my pajamas, and Hangman's House looked like the epitome of every house in those films.

I sighed deeply, and it was as if the house sighed with me. The inside wasn't any better than the outside. The scent of dust hung heavy in the stale air. I found the light switch next to the door and flicked it on.

"Figures," I grumbled and started across the room for the window.

The power was on, but the lights were dull. Even with them on, it was still gloomy and dark in the room.

I grabbed hold of the thick velvet drapes and yanked them apart. Sunlight flooded the room, and made it look ten times worse.

I wanted to yank them closed again but figured that wouldn't do any good. There was no point in hiding from the reality of the house. I tried not to think of the house as a metaphor for my life, but the idea didn't escape me. Sometimes I wished I could pull the drapes closed and hide from the mess my life had become as well. But just like with Hangman's House, it wouldn't do any good.

The room next to the living room was a dining room with a large table. It was covered in a worn tablecloth that had probably been very beautiful and expensive at one time. A large silver candelabra sat in the middle of the table. It needed a good polish as the metal was quite tarnished. There were half-melted black candles in each of the candelabra's cups. I thought that was a little odd, but I figured maybe my Great-Aunt Maude had just run out of regular candles the last time she used the candleholder.

The windows in the dining room were etched and the long white curtains looked moth-eaten. Wallpaper peeled off the walls, and the floor groaned with every step.

My next stop was the kitchen. It wasn't dirty beyond a thick layer of dust. Inside the pantry I found shelves full of decades-old cans and boxes of dry goods. Mice had gotten into the boxes and made a huge mess on the floor.

The appliances were old, and when I approached the refrigerator to open it, I heard a disconcerting rattling sound. The stove didn't appear to be in any better shape.

"I won't be able to cook anything in here without some major upgrades," I said and turned to leave.

As I did, a door caught my eye. It wasn't the back door to the house. I figured the door I'd missed before had to lead to a basement or cellar.

"No thank you. I'm not in the mood for a creepy basement just now. Maybe later."

I made my way back through the dining room and out into the living room. On the far wall from the dining room was a staircase. Nothing about the house made me believe it was going to be inhabitable without some major renovations, but I figured I should look around the upstairs anyway.

The stairs leading to the second level were only slightly more robust than those outside. I figured they weren't as weathered because being inside protected them. I stepped on the first riser to test it, and my theory proved true. It didn't even squeak when I put my full weight on it. The ones in the middle did, but not so much that I thought I'd fall through.

Upstairs was even dustier than the downstairs, if that was possible. The hallway area was dim, but the three bedroom doors were open and light from the outside streamed in since upstairs someone had left the drapes open in all the rooms. The light didn't quite make it to the hallway, and in fact, I noted that the light seemed to stop at the doorframes as if it were afraid to leave the rooms. I thought that was curious, but reasoned that it must have been a trick of the light or something to do with the architecture.

I looked up and saw that there was an attic door above me. It had one of those pull chains you used to pull the staircase down. I wasn't any more interested in going into the attic than I was the basement. So I checked out the bedrooms instead.

The linens were all still on the beds. They'd need to be washed, if they could be saved. I had linens for one bedroom in my things, so at least if the beds weren't in horrible condition, I'd be able to use one of the rooms as my bedroom while I stayed in Hangman's House. If I could make one room livable, then I didn't need to worry too much about having guest rooms. It wasn't like I was going to have any overnight visitors.

If I could get the biggest bedroom in shape, that was the one I wanted to use as my room. Not just because it was the biggest, but that was certainly a factor. It also had the most natural light because of the huge picture window and two side windows. There was also a lot of storage, which I thought was important even though I was fairly basic and didn't have much to put in the closet, massive armoire, or oak dressers.

I crossed the room to the door that I assumed was the closet. No sooner had I turned the knob and opened the door and I was running out of the room, down the stairs, and out onto the front lawn shrieking at the top of my lungs. Thank goodness there weren't very many close neighbors or they probably would have called the cops on me.

As soon as I was done pumping my legs while jogging in place and frantically running my hands through my hair while shaking my head, I began to laugh at myself. The bat in that closet had scared the ever-loving snot out of me, but I'd terrified the little guy too. He, or she, was long gone and not in my hair.

I decided at that point that it was time to give up on the house for the night. After I unhooked the trailer, I got back into the car and pulled it through the barest patch of grass and onto the street in front of the house.

In the city I never would have left a trailer full of my belongings just sitting out like that, even if it was locked, but I'd heard you could leave your doors unlocked in a small town without worrying. So I assumed my U-Haul full of stuff nobody probably wanted anyway would be fine.

I'd passed a place called Mama Hattie's on the way through town. There was a sign out front that said "rooms for rent", and I hadn't seen anything else that resembled a hotel or bed and breakfast. I Googled the number and gave them a call.

A woman answered the phone and confirmed that they did have an opening. I told her I'd be there in a few minutes. After that, I put the car in drive again, gave Hangman's House a wave, and drove off back in the direction I came. I wasn't looking forward to what I'd have to do to get Hangman's House livable, but honestly, it wasn't like I had anything better to do.

Mama Hattie's was a big house that I'd assumed had been converted into a bed and breakfast or at least single rooms to rent. When I walked inside to check in, I found a nearly empty room with just an old desk mostly blocking a door to another room. No one was around, but I decided to wait for a moment.

A long minute later, a young woman emerged from the room behind the desk. "Hello," she said and opened a book that sat on the desk. "I'm Cassidy, welcome to Mama Hattie's."

I was about to tell her that I'd just spoken to her on the phone when someone called out to her from the back room. "Cassidy, I swear to Pete, you are using too much soap in the towels again. I've told you it's a waste and that half a cap gets them clean enough. I swear you'd forget your own head if it wasn't attached."

Cassidy's cheeks colored with embarrassment, and I flashed her a sympathetic smile. "We spoke on the phone a few minutes ago. You said there is a room available."

"Oh, sure. It's seventy-five per night. If you want it, sign your name here," she said and pointed to a line in the ledger book she'd opened. "We take cash only. If you don't have any on you, there's an ATM at Mann's Gas & Grocery."

"I have it, but really? Seventy-five per night?" I said.

"Yeah, there aren't any other hotels around," Cassidy said with a shrug, and I got her meaning. Mama Hattie could get away with that price because out-of-town visitors had no other choice.

"Okay," I said. "Maybe if I can manage to only stay one night it won't blow my budget too much."

"Great, sign here," Cassidy said and pointed at the line in the ledger again. "I'll get the key."

Cassidy came back with the key and motioned for me to follow her. We walked through the kitchen to a door that lead downstairs. I sneezed twice because the scent of lavender and baby powder nearly overwhelmed me.

"The room's in the basement?" I asked as I rubbed my nose. "Don't you have anything upstairs?"

"Both rooms are in the basement. Yours is the one on the right. Let me know if you need anything else. Dinner is served in an hour. It's included in the price of the room."

"Thank you," I said and took the key.

I wanted to say that a free dinner didn't make up for a seventy-five-dollar basement room, but I figured I should just keep my trap shut. Complaining wasn't going to do any good. It was what it was.

I let myself into the room and found myself completely underwhelmed again. The exposed concrete brick walls of the basement room had been painted yellow, but the paint was chipping and flaking. The space was cramped, dark, and the air was heavy with dust and humidity. Not a good combination.

I put my bag on top of the small dresser that was just inside the door and then sat down on the bed. It creaked and groaned, and I got poked in the butt cheek by a spring. If Mama Hattie's was the only place to rent a room in Coventry, I needed to get Hangman's House livable ASAP.

What I needed was a plan. No, scratch that, what I needed was a group of big strong men who would work for free. No, scratch that too. What I needed was to not have been let go from my job. And not to have gotten divorced. And not to have had my ex get remarried a few months later. And for my ex and his new wife to not be expecting a baby after three months of being married when he and I had tried for years.

"No," I said and stood up. "Stop doing this to yourself, Brighton."

I didn't have a plan for Hangman's House or my life. Winging it was the best I could do.

After a shower and some clean clothes, I felt somewhat better. Having dinner with Mama Hattie and whoever was staying in the other room didn't sound like my kind of night, but again, I didn't have many other choices. I couldn't cook for myself until I moved back into Hangman's House, and springing for a meal at a restaurant when dinner was included in my room price was completely irresponsible.

I put my hair, still damp from my shower, up in a bun on top of my head. If I didn't, my wavy chestnut locks would probably go rogue on me. It was normally well behaved, but the humidity in the basement was enough that the frizz had begun to take hold.

Hattie, at least that's who I assumed she was, was already seated at the table when I got to the dining room. Cassidy was running around trying to get the food on the table.

"Can I help you, Cassidy?" I offered even though I was a guest. I hated seeing her look so flushed and flustered.

"She can handle it," the woman at the table said. "Can't you?"

"Yes, Hattie," Cassidy said.

I realized the overwhelming smell of baby powder and lavender was coming from Hattie. I sneezed again, but at least I knew she couldn't sneak up on anyone. Not that I had any reason to believe she'd be sneaking up on people, but she kind of gave off a vibe. Plus, she was the kind of person who chastised her employee for using too much soap to clean the towels. I for one, after having taken a shower, was happy with the amount of soap Cassidy had used, and I vowed not to stay long enough to have to use one cleaned to Hattie's "standards".

After a couple of minutes of awkward silence, a man came up from the basement and glared at me. "I usually sit there," he said coldly.

"Oh, sorry," I said and stood up.

I could have sworn I heard Hattie chuckle, but I couldn't be sure. I started to move to another chair.

"No, that's fine. You're there now. I'll just sit at another spot," he said and sighed.

"Really, I can move," I said.

"No, it's fine," he said and plopped down into a chair two down from Hattie. "I'm already comfortable."

"Okay," I responded and swore I heard Hattie chuckle again. "I didn't know, I'm sorry."

"Well, now you do," he scoffed. "I'm Professor Max Harkin," he said in a tone that told me I was supposed to know who that was.

But I didn't. I had no idea who he was.

"I'm Brighton Longfield," I said. "What are you a professor of?"

People liked when you asked them about themselves. I figured that would smooth over our rough introduction.

"I'm surprised you haven't heard of me," he sneered. "Most people who have any interest in the paranormal have heard of me."

"Well, that would explain it," I said. "I'm not particularly interested in the paranormal."

Hattie gasped and Cassidy dropped the gravy bowl she'd been setting on the table. It fell the last inch and tipped precariously, but did not spill more than a few drops. Cassidy made a weird sound like she was trying to stifle a laugh. She hightailed it out of the room and I thought I might have heard her belting out laughter in the kitchen.

Professor Max Harkin turned bright red, and I couldn't tell if it was from embarrassment or anger. "What are you doing in Coventry if you're not interested in the paranormal?" he huffed.

"I inherited my great-aunt's house. Hangman's House. Have you heard of it? And I'm not sure what the paranormal has to do with Coventry. I mean, my aunt believed in that stuff, but she was a few bricks short of a wall. I loved her to pieces, but she was off her rocker."

"She's off her rocker because she believes in the paranormal?" Professor Harkin asked, and I could tell I'd hit a nerve.

"No offense," I said with a shrug. "Some things are just a fantasy, and my great-aunt's took over her life. Not that I'm saying yours have too," I said and bit my lip.

"Young lady, I am a professor of parapsychology. I work for an actual university doing real science. What is it you do?"

"I'm just here to restore Hangman's House. Before that I worked in a call center. Nothing so esteemed as being a professor of parapsychology." The last part came out a bit snarkier than I'd intended.

"Well, I can see how that makes you an expert in the paranormal," he said with a snort. "I, on the other hand, have been collecting data and evidence for decades. I've also helped dozens of people and families rid themselves of nasty hauntings that were impacting the quality of their lives."

"Oh," was my response.

"Oh?"

"You take people's money for ghostbusting," I said and bit my lower lip hard because I was seconds away from calling him a total fraud and grifter. "It's just that if you'd collected data and evidence for decades as you say, I would have thought you'd have proved the existence of the paranormal already."

After that, he wouldn't even look at me. I supposed that was for the best. I could tell he was one of those professors that thought he was smarter than everyone in the room, and he wanted to make sure you knew it too.

I ate quickly and then retreated to my room in the basement. All through dinner, at least the part I was still around for, Professor Max Harkin made a show of telling Hattie and Cassidy his most regaling tales of saving families from evil hauntings. Interestingly enough, both women looked completely bored and detached despite Harkin's theatrics. I wondered if it was because he'd already told those stories a million times. He struck me as that type.

Back in my room, the stress of the day finally hit me. All I wanted to do was crash into bed. I was suddenly so tired that I didn't care if the bed was lumpy or pokey. Crawling under the covers in my dusty, dank room sounded fine by me.

Since the room was in the basement, there was only one narrow horizontal window on the outside wall at ground level. There were blinds covering it, but they were still open. I was too short to grasp the wand to close them, and I didn't have the will to start climbing on furniture to reach. I reasoned that no one was going to get down on their belly to look in my window anyway, and just left them alone as I crawled into bed.

Chapter Two

The first thing I noticed when I woke up the next morning was that those blinds were closed. I figured that I must have gotten up in the night to close them. While I had no recollection of doing it, I reasoned that perhaps the moonlight had woken me just enough to be annoyed. I shrugged it off and climbed out of the creaking bed.

I rubbed my hip gingerly where a mattress spring had poked it all night, and headed for the shower. Nothing in my room was disturbed. I laughed at myself for even considering that someone might have broken into my room in the night stealthily enough not to wake me and closed my blinds for me.

After I'd dressed and packed my things back into my bag, I stood at the door and listened for a moment. The last thing I wanted was to run into Harkin again. When I was satisfied that he wasn't in the hallway, I opened the door a crack and peeked out. The coast was clear so I hurried out of the room and darted up the stairs.

"There's no breakfast," Cassidy said when she noticed me hesitating in the kitchen. "But I made sandwiches. I can put one in a bag for you. Just don't tell Hattie. She'd have a fit if she knew I was giving away sandwiches."

I almost turned her down, but I knew it would be a mistake to go to the house with nothing to eat. "Sure, as long as it doesn't get you into trouble."

The distraction was welcome as I could hear Harking and Mama Hattie talking out in the room that served as the lobby. A few moments later, Cassidy handed me a stuffed brown paper lunch sack.

"Just a sandwich?" I asked with a smile.

"Shh," she said with one finger up to her lips.

"I need to check out," I said. "This place is a little rich for my blood, though I do appreciate everything you've done. I'm going to do my best to get Hangman's House livable today."

We walked into the living room area, and Cassidy stood behind the desk. "Well, come back any time if you need a place to stay," she said with a smile. "But I highly recommend not coming back if you can avoid it." She leaned across the desk and whispered that part. "Sign here where it says departure."

During the short drive back to Hangman's House, I regretted not asking Harkin if he was in Coventry studying some sort of paranormal phenomenon. Not that it mattered. He was a fraud and anything he was investigating wasn't real, but all the same, I kind of wished I knew why he was in town.

I pulled into the driveway and parked behind the trailer. I'd have to drive around the U-Haul again when I hitched it up to return it, but I loathed to do any more damage to the already pathetic grass.

My first inclination was to take everything inside so I could return the trailer, but I

decided to leave it for one more day. I
had to make sure that I could actually
make the house livable before I carried
everything in. Otherwise, I'd be stuck
moving things twice.

What I did need was my cleaning supplies.
I'd packed them last because I knew no
one had lived in Hangman's House for a
long time and it would need a thorough
cleaning. I just hoped that was all it
needed, but I had my doubts.

I opened the door to the back of the U-
Haul and grabbed my bucket full of
cleaning products as well as my trusty mop
and broom.

When I paused at the front door, I looked
up through narrowed eyes at the sign that
said "Hangman's House". The name was
creepy, and who knew why my family had
called the place that? It was one of the
first big changes I wanted to make. I'd
have to take that sign down and probably
put up another. That task had to wait until
after cleaning. I could live in the house with

a creepy name, but I couldn't live there if it was still an uninhabitable mess.

I'd like to have been able to say the morning flew by, but it didn't. After I'd thrown open the drapes and opened all the windows, I donned a filter mask and got down to the business of ridding Hangman's House of years of dust.

The utilities were on, thanks to a call and hefty deposits before I arrived, so I took the chance of plugging in an old Electrolux vacuum I found in the closet. I'd heard the older models lasted forever, and it was true. The lights flickered ominously the first time I threw the switch, but after that, it seemed that the house accepted my use of its juice.

I began to find that with a little dusting and scrubbing, Hangman's House wasn't as bad as I'd thought. It had just been neglected. Parts of the house where I could have sworn I'd seen potential structural issues and black mold were just dirty. Every moment I spent vacuuming up dust bunnies or scrubbing floors and counters with lemon-scented cleaner seemed to breathe new life into the house. If I'd believed in magic, I would have sworn that the lemon cleaner was some sort of potion. It was amazing what a little spit and polish could do.

I'd even made my first trip to the basement where I found an old washer and dryer at the bottom of the stairs. They were old, but they still worked, so I stripped the windows of the drapes and began running loads of laundry. I didn't venture any farther into the basement than the foot of the stairs where the machines were located, though. That was an adventure into the dark for another time.

At some point, my stomach sent out a loud protest. Cassidy had sent two sandwiches, a single serve bag of cheddar and sour cream potato chips, three chocolate chip cookies, and two bottles of water. Unfortunately, I'd polished it all off already. The work I was doing was hard, and I'd burned through the food with my morning work.

I looked at the clock and saw that it was coming up on afternoon. Stopping before the work was done didn't appeal to me, but neither did missing dinner because I didn't go to the store before it closed. My stomach rumbled loudly again, and I knew I wasn't going to be able to ignore it.

"Okay," I said. "I'll go to the store."

I quickly emptied out my bucket of water and put the Electrolux back in the closet. It was kind of a nice day out and I regretted that I didn't have time for a leisurely stroll into town. But my new home was on the outskirts of Coventry, so I didn't have time to walk.

As far as I could tell, Mann's Gas & Grocery was the only place in town to buy both gas and groceries. I pulled my car into a spot on the grocery side and made my way into the store.

It was a small store and it didn't carry nearly as many products as the store where I used to shop. I figured that was probably okay, though. I ate too much packaged garbage anyway.

I made my way around looking for things that were easy to cook like a bag of potatoes and a dozen eggs. I found some ground beef and hamburger buns too before looking for the soda aisle. I was about at the point where I would have killed someone for a Diet Coke. Not literally. Maybe literally.

When I was at one end of the soda aisle, two women came around the corner and stopped at the other end. The kept glancing over at me and whispering to each other. I caught what I thought was them saying the name Harkin, but I couldn't make out anything else.

I grabbed a twelve-pack of Diet Coke that I really couldn't afford but I swore that I'd ration it out, and started to leave the aisle. Before I could get very far, I heard one of the women call out to me. She shuffled up the aisle toward me with the other woman following behind at a distance.

"Hello," she said in a tone that sounded like artificial sweetener.

"Hello." I stopped and turned back around to face the woman.

"I don't recognize you, dear," she said. "You must be new in town."

"I'm Brighton Longfield. I just moved to town. My family is from Coventry, though," I said.

"Longfield, huh?" The woman seemed to be chewing the name over. "I can't say I recognize that name."

"Ah, well, my Great-Aunt Maude Tuttlesmith left me Hangman's House. I've just moved in," I said. "It's nice to meet you. I didn't catch your name."

But the woman didn't say anything else. Her eyes grew dark and she pursed her lips together before pushing past me and rushing away. The other woman shrugged her shoulders and quickly left in the other direction as well.

I thought the whole thing was strange, but I tried to brush it off. Perhaps the woman knew Maude from back before she was institutionalized. I'm sure she didn't make many friends with all of her rantings about witches, magic, and spirit conjuring. There wasn't much I could do but pay for my groceries and head back to Hangman's House to finish my work.

When I checked out, I noticed a few people were staring at me as they pointed and whispered. Instead of letting it make me paranoid, I ignored it and took my groceries out to the car.

A store across the street, Prue's Chocolate Treasures, caught my attention. I didn't have money to blow, but I really wanted some homemade candy. I promised myself that I'd only spend a couple of dollars as I crossed the street to the shop.

I only made it about halfway across the street when the delicious scent of sugar, chocolate, and fruit hit my senses. It was one of the most delicious and intoxicating scents I'd ever had the pleasure to smell. It felt like a siren song intended to lure you into its clutches, but it was so sweet that I wanted to be lured. I drifted across the street with a new smile on my face and took in the candy fragrance one more time before I pulled the door open.

Inside, that same sweet perfection felt like it had wrapped its loving arms around me. Everything about Prue's Chocolate

Treasures felt like a warm hug. The lights were soft but not dim. The décor was pastel but not childlike. There were murals painted on the walls of unicorns, rainbows, and clouds, but they were not cartoony. It was some serious artwork. The tables were round and each one was the color of a different flavor of saltwater taffy, and at the same time, they looked like something out of a high-art furniture catalog. The place just had a glow to it.

I wished I had more than a couple of dollars to spend in the shop, but I knew as soon as I found a way to make a living in Coventry, I'd be a regular at Prue's. The soft cozy feeling of the shop was completely shattered when I saw who was waiting at the head of the line.

Harkin was there in front of the glass pointing at the strawberry nougats. Then the woman behind the counter, who I assumed was Prue, was putting them in a little pink box. She had a huge smile on her face, and I had to wonder if she was just really good at customer service or if she knew a side of Harkin I hadn't seen. Or maybe she just really liked jerks?

The more I watched, the more I got the feeling that it wasn't good customer service. She had blush to her cheeks, and I could swear that the woman was batting her eyelashes.

They moved down the line from standing in front of the glass case to the counter near the register. Prue, or who I assumed was Prue, was about to hand Harkin the box but instead, she set it down and leaned toward him a little.

She smiled sweetly again and he leaned in a little too. I found myself drifting forward so that I could hear their exchange. It wasn't that I wanted to be a creepy eavesdropper, but I found myself drawn into her enthusiasm for whatever she was about to tell Harkin.

There was something about her, and I guessed she had that effect on a lot of people. The woman I assumed was Prue was what I would have considered a plus-sized beauty queen. She reminded me of that model that had become really popular. Angela? Ashley? It was something like that. Either way, Prue was just as beautiful and had a ton of charisma too. She was zaftig, and I could tell she had confidence in her curves. She did. Until...

"So, Professor," she practically purred. "You've been coming in here a lot while you've been in town. I was just wondering if there was something I could interest you in other than the strawberry nougats. I thought that perhaps you might be interested in dinner or maybe a drink?"

I didn't understand why she would want to go out with him, but I admired her spirit. Maybe it's just that she didn't know him that well because she'd only interacted with him in the shop. He wasn't a bad-looking man, but he was full of himself. I didn't realize how full until he started laughing at her.

He laughed at her.

"Prue, don't be stupid," he said when he got control of his amusement, and I felt my blood boil for her. "You know that someone like me would never settle for someone your... size. I was really only here for the strawberry nougats. I'm sure you understand as you appear to be a big, big fan of your own wares." And then he began chuckling again like he'd just let us all in on the world's funniest joke.

Prue turned three shades of red before tears began running down her cheeks. The other two customers in the store with me just stood there with their mouths hanging agape like mine. We waited for something to happen.

She looked like she was about to say something, but instead, Prue just turned and ran into the back. I didn't blame her. That jerk had just humiliated her in front of her customers. If he wasn't interested in her, that was fine, but he didn't have to be cruel about it.

I wanted to go comfort her. Prue's sadness drew me in the same way her lighthearted charisma had, but I didn't know her. I wasn't sure she'd want a total stranger walking into the back of her shop uninvited to witness her crying in humiliation, so I stayed there in line.

A few minutes passed, and she didn't come back out. I glared at Harkin when he spoke. The jerk had the nerve to still be standing there waiting for Prue to come ring up his candy.

"There's no one here to ring up my nougats," he said. "The service in this place is really going downhill."

That was it. I had to go. I noticed on the way back to my car that the other two customers left the shop shortly after me. Harkin left as I was starting the engine. He didn't have his box of nougats.

I drove straight home after that. When I was getting my groceries out of the backseat of the car, I noticed a black cat sitting on my doorstep. Well, calling him a black cat didn't do him justice. He was far more like a mini panther. I'd never seen a housecat that huge before. His fur was thick and shone beautifully in the late afternoon sun. He was beautiful and obviously well-taken care of, and that made me wonder why he was sitting outside my front door as if he expected me to let him in.

After shooing him away, I went inside and put my groceries on the counter. I probably should have checked to make sure the refrigerator worked properly before I bought perishable groceries, but fortunately it seemed to work fine. I quickly sprayed the inside and shelves with lemon kitchen cleaner, wiped them down, and then put my food away. Another spritz of the cleaning solution on the outside and a wipe down later, and I noticed the appliance stopped making the slightly annoying buzzing sound it had been making since my first visit to Hangman's House.

"Huh," I said. "Is that all you wanted?"

I shook my head and chuckled at the fact that I'd just asked my refrigerator a question and moved on to put the rest of my groceries in the empty cabinets. I wanted to just leave the bags with the non-perishables on the counter, but I knew if I did, they'd sit there forever. I'd just take what I needed out of the bags and then eventually throw them away when they were empty.

My ex hated that. He'd chastise me all of the time for not putting everything away, but it wasn't like he ever helped me with the shopping or the cooking.

Donnie always acted like him making more money was enough. He didn't even acknowledge that I also worked full-time. It was probably better that we never had a child, and I felt a little bad for his new wife.

"Not my circus. Not my monkeys," I reminded myself.

I went upstairs to the bedroom that I planned to use as mine. I needed to get it clean and ready if I was going to stay at Hangman's House that night. Before I stripped the beds, I checked the closet for any bats, I was prepared to flee again, but I found none.

I stripped the bed and put the linens in a laundry basket I'd found in the basement next to the washer and dryer. My biggest fear had been that the mattress would be in unusable condition. After all, the beds had to be decades old. But interestingly enough, it looked pretty new. It was definitely in better shape than the one I'd spent the night on at Mama Hattie's. I took the linens downstairs to the basement and put them in the washer after moving its load to the dryer.

When I got back to the bedroom, I could swear the mattress looked even better. It was whiter and there seemed to be less dust on the headboard too.

"Must be a trick of the light," I said and reached into the box next to the bed for the sheets I'd brought.

Once the bed was made with my sheets and comforter, I retrieved the Electrolux and vacuumed the floor.

It appeared that the room had undergone an amazing transformation. I couldn't believe what a little vacuuming and some clean sheets had done for a room that had scared me away the first night. When I looked up, I could swear the dark brown water stains in the ceiling had faded almost into oblivion. Still, I was convinced it was nothing more than funny lighting.

If nothing else, I was glad I hadn't given up on Hangman's House after my first impression. It had been completely wrong. I found some blinds in the bedroom closet and a toolbox and stepladder in the hall closet. It didn't take me long to hang them over the window, but I left them open so the light could fill the room. It still stopped at the doorway like it was afraid to go into the hall or something, but I reasoned, again, that it was just something in the angle of the house's position or something.

When I was done in the bedroom, I went downstairs and put the vacuum away again. A memory of Donnie tripping over the cord one time when I'd left a vacuum out at our old apartment tried to worm its way into my thoughts and spoil my good mood, but I didn't let it. But I was amazed at how much easier it was for me to clean and tidy when I was doing it for me instead of because I was scrambling to meet his standards.

The drapes in the living room needed to be put back, so I worked on that next. I decided that perching on the edge of an end table, like I'd done to take them down, wasn't the best idea. The house didn't have a garage, but I'd seen a shed out back. I decided to look there for a ladder, and I hit pay dirt. I also noted that the shed contained more tools, a lawn mower, and stuff like rakes, hoses, and gardening shears. It was nice to know I wouldn't have to buy all that stuff if my lawn decided to come back from the dead.

When I was just about done hanging the curtains, I noticed movement outside the front window. I peeked through the drawn drapes and saw that it was the cat again. He'd jumped up on the outside sill and was staring at me through the glass. I watched him for a second before saying "shoo" and waved him away. He looked at me for another moment and then put one of his big paws on the glass.

So I went outside and tried to shoo him away again. "You have to go, kitty," I said and tried to get him to jump off the sill. "You need to go home."

He did jump off the sill, but instead of moving along, he darted into the house through the front door that I'd left ajar. "Awesome," I said and followed him in.

The cat stretched out in front of the unlit fireplace that shared a wall with the dining room and kitchen. I couldn't help but notice that he sure seemed at home and figured that he must have been living in the empty house before I came along. I didn't want a cat, but I didn't want to pick him up and throw him out either. As far as I knew, Coventry didn't have an animal shelter. I didn't want to call county animal control or the sheriff about a cat breaking into my house. I decided I'd let him sleep there in front of the fireplace for one night and then figure out what to do with him later.

Chapter Three

The cat didn't just lay in front of the fireplace, though. When I went into the kitchen to make my dinner, he followed me at a distance. While I cooked a pan of ground beef and a pot of potatoes, he seemed to be studying me carefully. The scent of the cooking meat made my stomach rumble, and I guess it had the same effect on the cat. Each time I turned around, he was just a little bit closer.

"I guess you're thinking I'm going to share some of this beef with you," I said, and he raised his paw like he had before. "Oh, really?" I teased, but he just lay down and watched me some more. "This is my dinner."

When the food was done cooking, I'd committed to ignoring him. It didn't happen. I spooned some of the cooked beef into a bowl and set it on the floor next to another I'd filled with water.

"I'm not doing this because you're my cat," I said more to myself than the cat. "I'm doing it because it's impolite not to share your dinner with guests. You can't be my cat. I can barely handle my own life let alone be responsible for another living creature."

He meowed in response, and it vaguely sounded like a cat version of "thank you." But that was a trick of my tired mind and too many cat videos on social media. Not that I watched a lot of cat videos. I was totally not a cat person. I mean, I'd always wanted one when I was a little girl, but I'd grown out of that.

While the cat ate his food, I sat down at the kitchen table with my meal of boiled potatoes and ground beef. At least I had salt and pepper for them. I liked plain meals most of the time. It kept me humble, and it made life easier. I began to think of what Donnie would have said about a meal like the one I was eating, but I pushed those thoughts aside again. It was getting easier to let them go. I was proud of myself for that.

I knew my savings weren't going to last forever, but I had no prospects for a job in Coventry. I'd just have to make the money last as long as possible. Perhaps if things got dire, I could always do odd jobs. I could clean and the lawnmower in the garage meant I could cut grass for my neighbors too. That thought gave me a little comfort. It would probably make the teenagers of Coventry who depended on that type of work for pocket money hate me, but what could I do? I had to eat and keep the power on. Until I could figure out what to do with the cat, I had another mouth to feed too.

When I was done washing the few dishes I'd used, it wasn't very late yet, but I was exhausted. All I wanted to do was get the kitchen tidied up and then make my way to bed.

While I was putting the pans away, instead of leaving them in the drying rack, I noticed what looked like a jar on the top shelf of the cabinet. I probably should have gotten the ladder, but instead I climbed up on the counter to retrieve it. I got it off the shelf and climbed down as carefully as I could.

It was actually a porcelain canister with a little lid that sealed with rubber rings. When I opened it, I couldn't believe my luck. I pulled the slip of paper out first.

"*A little something for a rainy day*," the note inside read.

It must have been Maude's handwriting, but why had she left herself a note? I shrugged. She was the Mad Maude I loved after all. In addition to the note was a stack of five- and ten-dollar bills. A thick stack. All told it was just over five hundred dollars. That was enough money for me to eat and keep the power on for at least a couple of months. Maybe more if I was careful. The most interesting part, and it had to have been a total coincidence, was that when I took the money out of the canister, thunder cracked in the sky and it began to rain.

"That's a coincidence," I said to the cat. "But I guess I should pay this good fortune forward. You can stay with me. For now.

No promises, but let's go to bed. I'm tired."
I started to walk out of the kitchen to the
dining room, but I stopped and turned to
the cat again. "But you stay off my pillow."

I tucked myself into bed and my head
barely hit the pillow before I was out.
Despite being exhausted and the bed
being comfortable, I did not sleep
peacefully. I'd wake fitfully and find the
cat pressed against my back purring softly.
It was enough to help me drift off again,
but it wasn't enough to keep the night
terrors at bay. My dreams were terrible,
anxiety-ridden nightmarescapes.

The one I remember the most clearly was a
group of people in long dark robes shoving
me and a few other women around. I
couldn't see the faces of the people in the
robes because their heads were covered
with hoods. It was just blackness under their
cowls, but the strange thing was that I
couldn't see the faces of the women with
me either. I got the feeling that I knew
them somehow, but I couldn't focus on
their features.

We were all being shoved away from somewhere we wanted to be, but the others didn't want us anymore. It was heartbreaking and made me feel as though I was falling endlessly even though I stood upright in the dream.

When I woke up, the bedroom blinds were closed. It was odd because I'd left them open when I went to sleep. I liked the moonlight, and I didn't figure anyone could see in my second-story bedroom window anyway. Plus, I hadn't realized they were open until I already had myself tucked under the covers. I didn't want to move from my cocoon, so I'd left them alone.

Maybe there was just something wrong with the mechanism, I reasoned. They'd been stashed in the back of a closet, so it wasn't like they were brand new or anything. Perhaps the cat had messed with them in the night too. I'd seen plenty of videos of cats attacking blinds. Even if he had, it probably wouldn't have woken me. I was too dead tired, and it wasn't as if they'd been ripped down.

Still, the memory of Harkin prattling on about his paranormal investigations sprang to mind. He'd made it pretty clear that he thought something supernatural was going on in Coventry. I told myself that was silly, but for just a moment, the hair on the back of my neck stood up. A realization was swimming around in the dark waters of my subconscious mind, and it was just about to surface when the cat jumped up on the dresser and knocked off my deodorant and a bottle of lotion.

"Cat!" I yelled and jumped out of bed. "You're so evicted."

I chased him down the stairs and into the kitchen where he jumped on top of the refrigerator and yawned at me. His big green eyes stared at me with a knowing look that seemed too intense for an animal. Plus, he'd comforted me when I was having nightmares.

"Okay," I said. "I'm having eggs for breakfast, but I will heat up some of the leftover beef for you."

The cat sat patiently while I fried up two eggs and heated some leftover potatoes for myself. When that was done, I nuked his beef for a few seconds. He looked longingly at my eggs.

"Let me guess, you want one of my yolks," I said jokingly, but he put up his paw again. "That's a cool trick, but all right."

I used my fork to cut around the yolk on one of my eggs and then plopped it into his bowl. We ate breakfast together, and then I had to get back to work on the house. I still needed to spend some time in the dining room and the spare bedrooms. That and the bathtub needed a thorough cleaning so that I could shower when I was done with work that day. I was already getting pretty ripe, and I didn't want to go to bed dirty again.

After I'd done the dusting and vacuuming in the spare bedrooms and dining room, I finished the laundry and moved on to the upstairs bathroom. It was a bigger room than I would have expected. The clawfoot tub was huge, and I hoped that I could clean it up. I knew it would break my heart if it wasn't salvageable.

The cat curled up in the pedestal sink and watched me as I scoured and scrubbed. As much elbow grease as I put into cleaning that tub, I'd have to be careful that I didn't fall asleep in the bath. Of all the work I'd done, it was definitely the most physically taxing, but when I was finished, I clapped my hands with joy. Despite the fact that it was decades old, and before I began cleaning it, I thought it might be beyond repair, it looked brand new. All of the cracks in the porcelain had wiped away like they were streaks of dust and water and not actual cracks. The stains were gone too, and the hardware looked as though someone had installed it yesterday.

My stomach growled, and I realized it was getting close to dinnertime. I hadn't eaten since breakfast, and I did not feel like cooking again. While I was supposed to be careful with my money, I reasoned that one meal at the town's diner wouldn't kill my budget. I swore I'd get the special.

Whatever it was, as long as it was cheap and I didn't have to cook it, I'd enjoy every bite.

I wanted a long soak, but I also wanted to eat. So I compromised and only filled the tub halfway. While it filled, I heated up some more of my leftover beef for the cat. A quick bath, some fresh clothes, and I was ready to hit the town.

My car stayed in the driveway and I walked the mile or so to the town square. Dumbledore's Diner was the only restaurant I knew of in town. Apparently, the owners were super fans of a set of novels and movies about a certain kid wizard.

I walked inside and the place was packed. There was memorabilia everywhere, and the din of dozens of conversations made me feel oddly at ease. Maybe it was because no one turned around to look at me when I walked in. Perhaps I had become old news around town already.

"Ah, fresh meat," a man said as the door closed behind me.

I guess not.

"Stop it right now, John," a gorgeous woman with ebony skin and curly black hair said as she playfully slapped the man with a menu. "Welcome to Dumbledore's Diner. I'm Keisha, and that idiot is John," she said without a trace of malice in her voice.

"Hey, I might be the idiot, but you married me," he shot back. "What does that say about you?"

"That I have infinite patience." She smiled at him.

"That you do, my love. That you do."

"Anyway," Keisha said and turned her attention back to me. "We're glad you dropped in. We were hoping we wouldn't have to come out to Hangman's House and drag you out," she said with a chuckle. "We probably should have brought you a fruit basket or something, but as you can see, we have our hands full." Keisha waved to the crowd of diners.

"Is it always like this?" I asked.

"Breakfast, lunch, and dinner," she said. "Good thing we love it. Speaking of that, dinner is on us. It's the least we can do since we couldn't make it out to the house to welcome you."

"Thank you," I said as she handed me a menu.

"The only thing we'd ask if you mind sharing a table with someone?" John asked. "Otherwise it could be a while."

Right on cue, my stomach rumbled loudly. "I don't mind sharing at all."

"Great, right this way," Keisha said and beckoned for me to follow.

Keisha stopped a two-top table where a woman who I guessed was about my age sat studying a menu. "I don't know why I make myself look over the menu," the woman said without looking up at us. "I already know what I'm going to order."

"Hagrid's Haystack with a side of bacon?" Keisha asked.

"You know it." The woman handed Keisha the menu and finally took in that there was someone else standing beside her. "I heard your husband say there was fresh meat, but I didn't know you'd be bringing her to me," she said with a chuckle. "I'm Annika, and it looks like you're my date for the evening."

"Annika, this is Brighton, the new girl in town. We're packed tonight, and I was hoping you'd share your table."

"Of course. Please sit with me, Brighton," she said, and I did.

"It's nice to meet you," I said and opened the menu. "Looks like Hagrid's Haystack is a full stack of pancakes. I'll just have what she's having." I handed the menu back to Keisha.

"A woman after my own heart," Annika said as Keisha walked away. "You're going to love the pancakes here. They are so buttery with this crispy edge. They are to die for."

My stomach responded with a rumble. "I can't wait."

Red rose in my cheeks, and I was embarrassed at my body's protest. I don't know why I'd expected Annika to say something to embarrass me further, but she didn't. She flashed a knowing smile, and it put me at ease immediately.

"You won't have to wait long. The service here is outstanding. Plus, the haystack and bacon is one of the most popular specials. They keep them coming through the rush. It won't take but a few minutes. I always end up working through lunch and I'm devastatingly famished by dinnertime," Annika said and then switched gears. "So you moved into Hangman's House?"

I was about to ask her how she knew that, but then it dawned on me. "Small town."

"That it is. But I think it's great that you've moved there. It's such a neat old house, and it was a shame that it sat empty for so long."

"You've been inside?" I asked. Annika didn't look old enough to have been around before Great-Aunt Maude was sent off to the asylum. If she was, then she was a very young child when it happened.

"Yeah, it was a rite of passage in high school. The legend was that Mad Maude, sorry if that's offensive," she said, and that time her cheeks colored.

"It's not. She was a little mad, but I still loved her," I said. "But please tell me. Go on."

"Okay, so the legend was that Maude put a curse on the house to protect it from any Skeenbauers. So it's been a family tradition for at least a couple of generations for teenage Skeenbauers to sneak into Hangman's House on a full moon. If you spend the night, then it means you're..." She hesitated. "It means you're pure of heart or something. I can't remember exactly, it's been a decade."

"The Skeenbauers?"

"Oh, yeah," Annika said. "I'm Annika Skeenbauer. Our families, assuming you're related to Maude, have been locked in a feud for, like, ever."

"And do you believe in that stuff? I mean the curse, not the feud."

"Eh," she said with a shrug. "It is what it is. But I spent the night in the house, so either I'm pure of heart or it's just a legend. The house is really cool though. I hope you're able to bring it back to its former glory."

"It's not in as bad of shape as I thought when I got to town."

Before she could say anything else, Keisha delivered our pancakes and bacon. "I forgot to ask you if you wanted a drink," she said.

"A Diet Coke when you get the chance," I said.

"Be right back."

"I think we're going to get along just fine," Annika said as she picked up her glass and took a sip.

Keisha returned with a glass for me moments later. "I'll be back to check on you ladies in a bit."

"Thank you," Annika and I said in unison.

"To new friends and Diet Coke," Annika said and raised her glass.

We toasted, giggled, and then dug into our food. It must have been a day when Annika skipped lunch because she tore into her stack of pancakes as enthusiastically as I did.

Our conversation stopped while we ate, but I noticed that I felt completely at ease with Annika, something I never expected to feel with a stranger in an unfamiliar place.

Her phone was on the table face down, and I hadn't really noticed it until it began to vibrate. Annika finished chewing and took a swig of her drink before she picked it up and looked at the screen.

"I'm so sorry to be rude, but I have to take this. Do you want me to go outside?"

"No, it's okay," I said. "As long as you don't mind."

"Not at all. Please finish your food. Hopefully this is good news and a short call."

Annika answered the phone with an expectant hello. "This is she," she said, and then it seemed to go downhill from there.

I could hear the other person squawking, but I couldn't make out what they were saying. The call wasn't short, and from the look on Annika's face, it wasn't good news.

"Thank you," she said tersely and hung up.

For a moment, I wasn't sure what to do. "I guess I should ask you if everything is all right, but feel free to tell me to pound sand since you don't really know me."

"It's okay," she said. "That was just my insurance company. I've had some shoplifting going on in my store. I own Annika's Closet just off the square. It's a resale and vintage shop. Anyway, the insurance company isn't going to reimburse me for the value of a couple of things that were stolen. They don't think the items were worth what I know they were worth. So unless I get them back, I'm kind of up a creek over it."

"I'm sorry," I said.

"It's okay. I mean, it's not enough to put me out of business or anything, it's just kind of a bummer. But that's enough of my sob story," she said. "Why don't you tell me more..."

Her phone buzzing cut her off again. "I'm sorry," she said and looked at the screen again. "Man. It's my grandma. I've got to go. It was so nice meeting you. Can you meet me here tomorrow at noon for lunch?"

"Sure," I said.

Annika stood up and scooted out of the booth. It was then I noticed she was dressed in an eggplant sixties style sheath dress and white go-go boots. Her auburn hair was tied up in a high ponytail, and I

67

couldn't help but think she pulled the look off perfectly.

"Awesome sauce. I'll be here at noon on the dot. See you then," Annika said cheerfully. "Au revoir."

"Can I get you anything else?" Keisha asked moments later.

"No, I think I'm all done," I said. "Thank you so much for everything, and it was nice meeting you."

I left the diner feeling better than I had in months. Since I was going to be in Coventry for the foreseeable future, I decided to learn all of the shortcuts through town. To me, that just meant walking home a different way.

Coventry being a small town, there weren't really many other routes home, so I decided to cut through the alley behind Dumbledore's Diner. I was bebopping along thinking about how nice it would be to have a friend in town when I almost tripped over someone lying in the alley.

"Oh, my," I started. "Are you okay?"

I had my phone out to call 911 and was halfway bent over to check on the person before I realized that it was Harkin and he was dead. He was deader than dead. He was gray and his eyes were vacant, and suddenly I was almost screaming.

The hysterical shock and dread climbed to a fever pitch inside of me when a big black cat jumped onto my shoulder. The cat, my cat but *not* my cat, rubbed his face against my ear and purred softly.

I could clearly hear him begin to speak. "Brighton, you need to pull yourself together. Calm down and handle this like a big girl. I know you can do it."

It felt like I was in a trance when I dialed 911 and told the operator where I was and what I'd found, but I knew I wasn't. That was impossible. Not only could the cat not talk, but he certainly couldn't put me in a trance.

As I hung up the phone with the operator, I had that strange sensation again. It was like something was trying to surface in my mind. I started to wonder if Mad Maude was really so crazy. I wasn't dreaming, and I would swear under oath the cat just whispered to me.

What if all of her talk about magic, nodes, ley lines, and witchcraft weren't just the ramblings of a disturbed mind? Or maybe I was just as nuts as my great-aunt if I thought I heard the cat talking to me.

Chapter Four

I sat on the curb near the alley when the sheriff's cruiser pulled up. A stern but handsome-looking man in jeans and a black t-shirt stepped out of the car and walked toward me. I figured that he must have been off duty when the call came in because he wasn't in uniform. Either that or he was the killer and he'd stolen the sheriff's vehicle, but that was just my overactive imagination getting away from me. Making up a story in my head distracted me from the grim reality I'd stepped into after dinner.

To keep my mind off the dead body in the alley, I studied the sheriff's very much alive one as he approached me. Strong jaw, broad chest, big biceps. He was a walking *hunky, small-town sheriff* cliché with his wavy blond hair and intense blue eyes.

He ran a hand through that wavy hair before offering me a hand to help me to my feet. "Good evening, ma'am."

His hand was warm and comforting, though the electric sparks I half expected from reading too many romance novels did not materialize. "Thank you," I said as he pulled me to my feet.

"I'm Sheriff Thorn Wilson. I assume you're the person who made the 911 call."

"Oh, no. I just like hanging around dead bodies. I don't know who called it in," I said with a chuckle.

I instantly regretted making the joke because he did not laugh. In fact, all Sheriff Thorn Wilson did was narrow his eyes at me before pulling out a notepad and pen. I swallowed a lump in my throat as he scribbled something down.

"I was joking," I said, but it came out as kind of a high-pitched squeak, so I took a deep breath and tried to start again. "I'm Brighton Longfield. I just moved to town, so I'm new around here. And yes, I did make the call. He's back there in the alley." I pointed my thumb over my shoulder. "It's Professor Max Harkin."

"Wait here," Thorn said and brushed past me quickly.

I turned around and watched him walk up to Harkin's body. He knelt down and looked him over before standing back and walking in my direction again.

"Keep waiting," he said as he walked past and went to his car. "I'm going to talk to you after I call this in."

Thorn didn't even stop walking to speak to me, and I feared I'd made a terrible impression with my stupid joke. I didn't know what had possessed me to say something so horrible, but I could only guess it was my way of dealing with the stress of the situation.

He got in his cruiser and I watched him radio in the body. After a couple of minutes, he got back out of the car and came back to me.

"Ms. Longfield? Correct?" he asked.

"Yes, or you can call me Brighton."

"Okay, Brighton. How well did you know the victim?" he said and readied his pad and pen.

It was then that I realized that I was probably a suspect. I should have known that at least initially I would be, but I hadn't even thought about it. All I had to do was stay calm, tell him what I knew, and that would lead him to the real suspects. I was just the new girl in town who found a body.

"I didn't really know him well at all," I said because I didn't.

"But you knew who he was despite only being in town for a couple of days."

"Well, yes. In that couple of days, I've had two rather unpleasant run-ins with Professor Harkin." That statement probably made me look even more like a suspect, but it was the truth. I had nothing to hide, I reminded myself.

"Why don't you tell me about that." Sheriff Wilson put the tip of his pen to his pad and prepared to write.

So I proceeded to fill him in on the details of my stay at Mama Hattie's and dealing with Harkin at dinner. After that, I told him about witnessing Harkin's cruel rejection of Prue in her candy store. He listened the whole time and took notes while nodding his head.

"I'm going to need you to stick around town for now," he said. "You said that you just moved to town? You don't need to travel for the move right now, do you?"

"Yes, I inherited Hangman's House when my Great-Aunt Maude died, and I've just recently decided to move in. I'm not going back to where I came from. I do need to take my U-Haul back."

If I wasn't mistaken, he seemed a little stunned, but he didn't say anything to explain his surprise. All Thorn said was, "Just don't go anywhere since you're part of an active investigation. Okay?"

"I understand," I said. "I can go?"

"Yes, I think it would be better if you cleared out before the coroner gets here," he said. "Hey, before you go, I can send one of my deputies over to take that U-Haul back for you."

"You think I'm that much of a flight risk that I'll try to abscond when I return my moving trailer?"

"No, I think this is a small town and we help out when we can. It's one of the benefits of living in Coventry," he said, and I could swear he almost cracked a smile.

"I'll take you up on your hospitality, then. Have a good night, Sheriff," I said. "And thank you."

"You do the same, ma'am. And you're welcome."

The thing he said about me being part of an active investigation sounded ominous. "He must suspect that I killed Harkin," I said to the cat who was strolling next to me as we make our way home. "And I don't know if I buy that returning my U-Haul is just small-town hospitality. He must think I'll try to run off or something."

"Telling you that was just standard operating procedure, Brighton. It doesn't mean that you're an actual suspect. Besides, you didn't do it, so there's not going to be any evidence linking you to his death," the cat responded. "And it is small-town hospitality. Not everyone is Coventry is so friendly, but Thorn is one of the good guys."

"That should make me feel better, but it doesn't. This whole thing makes me anxious. Plus, I almost tripped over a dead body. That's pretty gross."

I stopped chatting and stared straight ahead when I realized that I was talking to the cat. My breathing became shallow when it further occurred to me that I'd very vividly imagined him answering me.

"It's going to be all right," the cat said.

"I'm so going nuts. I'm going to end up in the asylum like Maude," I said to myself and not the cat. "These things run in families. And now I'm talking to myself."

"I'm not going anywhere just because you feel like you need to pretend like you can't hear me," the cat said. "We're in this together for reasons that are going to become clear soon."

I reached the edge of my yard and hurried toward the front door. After I practically leapt up the steps, I paused at door. As turned the knob and walked through, I felt a chill run down my spine. Again, I was on the verge of some sort of realization, but it completely fizzled once I was inside. I decided that it must have been stress-induced anxiety from finding a dead body.

One thing was for sure, I felt like I needed a proper bath after spending time in the alley with a dead body. Even if I didn't touch it and I was only in the alley for a minute, it felt like some of the ick had seeped into me. So I ran a tub of hot water and poured in some of my favorite lavender relaxation bubble bath.

I was just relaxing in the tub trying to clear my mind when the cat jumped up on the counter and knocked the bottle of bubble bath on the floor. "Hey," I scolded, but then I glanced at my phone and realized that what I'd thought was just a minute was nearly a half hour. I'd almost fallen asleep in the tub, and the cat had saved me. "Sorry," I said as I pushed myself to my feet.

It had been a long day, and what I needed most was to get to bed. After drying off, I opened the blinds to the room and put on my pajamas. The bed looked warm and inviting, but I was afraid I'd lie awake thinking about Harkin.

Those fears were unfounded, though. The weight of the day pressed on my eyelids, and soon enough, I was ready to drift off again. Seconds before sleep took me, the cat jumped up on my pillow.

"Hey," I said. "I'm thankful that you saved me from drowning in the bathtub and all, but I said you had to stay off my pillow, cat."

"My name is not cat," he said haughtily. "My name is Merimus, but you may call me Meri if it suits you. I am the Tuttlesmith family familiar, and I am at your service, Brighton. But I would prefer to be called by my name and not *cat*."

"I'm dreaming," I said and scrunched my eyes closed as tight as I could. "I have to be dreaming."

"You're not dreaming and, Brighton, I'm talking to you. Closing your eyes isn't going to stop you from hearing me."

So I grabbed the covers and pulled them up over my head. "I don't want to be crazy. I don't want to live in an institution," I mumbled to myself.

"You don't need to go to an institution, Brighton. You're not crazy, and neither was Maude," Meri said. "She was the best of the Tuttlesmith witches, and that scared the wrong people."

I tossed the covers back and sat up in the bed with my legs crossed. "You need to stop talking because cats cannot talk," I said. "You cannot talk, and I cannot hear you. I just need to get some sleep."

"You can hear me and let me tell you a little bit about why," Meri began. "I'm a familiar. That means that I'm like your magical assistant. That's the easiest way for me to explain it. I'm not a witch, and I never was, but you are. Your entire family is. Maude was too. She wasn't mad at all, and I'm sure if you think back very hard you can remember her talking about her cat or you'll remember seeing pictures of her with me in them. Think hard, Brighton."

I was about to put my fingers in my ears and start singing when I recalled a picture my grandmother had shown me of Maude when she was much younger. Maude did have a big black cat named Meri. When I was little, I'd always assumed it was a girl named Mary, though.

"No," I said. "It just can't be."

"It is, and I am in your service. At one time, I was the familiar for the Skeenbauer witches, but I might have dropped a house on one of them or something by accident. It's hard to recall," he said and swished his tail as if to sweep the memory away.

"Either way, they cursed me to serve the Tuttlesmith family for eternity. The only way I'll ever be free of my service to your family is if the last Tuttlesmith or Skeenbauer witch dies. They were my family, but now you're my family. Which I am totally thrilled about. No really, it's amazing."

"You're kind of snarky," I said. "Wait, Skeenbauer? That's Annika's last name. So she's a witch and I'm a witch, and our families are involved in some sort of witch feud? And you were their familiar, but they cursed you and sent you away? That's terrible. I'm so sorry."

I felt very bad for him. Being cast out when you were no longer useful was a feeling I could identify with wholeheartedly.

"That's the very abbreviated version," Meri responded.

"Well, it's going to stay abbreviated because I'm going to sleep, and when I wake up, I'll realize this was all a very sad but realistic dream. Because cats can't talk, and witches don't exist."

I lay down, rolled over and pulled the covers up over my head again. I heard Meri make a *tsking* sound, but he settled down against my back again. I stared out through the open blinds for a few minutes trying to make sense of what was going on, but sleep won quickly as I drifted off.

Chapter Five

When I woke up, the blinds were closed
again. I was sure I hadn't gotten out of
bed all night, because the cat and I were
in the exact same positions as when I fell
asleep. A feeling I couldn't quite explain
crept up my spine. It was as if I'd thought
the world was in focus, but now I could see
that it was a little off-kilter. Either that or I
was worried that there was someone
secretly living in my house that liked to
close the blinds while I slept. Oh, and
they'd broken into my room at Hattie's to
close them there too.

What I needed was some answers, and
hopefully they didn't end with me being
completely nuts. I stood up from my bed
and planted my feet on the floor as
another new idea hit me. This one was as if
there was a tiny itch in the back of my
brain. Hangman's House wasn't what it
appeared to be.

I'd seen it as just another old house, but it was like I'd connected with it in a deeper way. There was so much more, and all I had to do was open my eyes and look. I had no idea where these thoughts were coming from, but it was almost as if they radiated up from the floorboards, traveled up my body, and then lodged themselves in my brain. Just like everything else, it was crazy, but it felt like the house had established a telepathic link straight to my mind. Could houses even think?

I stepped out into the hallway and looked around. Nothing seemed any different, but as I was about to write off my feelings as being more craziness, my eyes drifted up to the pull chain that would grant me access to the attic.

The chain stuck at first, but two good, hard yanks and the stairs came down with a loud creaking sound. "Let's do this," I said to Meri without really considering that I was talking to him again. "But I guess you already know what's up here."

At the top of the stairs I felt along the wall until I found a switch. I almost fell backwards down the steps when the light came on, and I saw what was in the attic.

"Get out," I whispered. "You've got to be kidding me."

"Nope, it's real."

"You're talking again and it's freaking me out," I said to Meri without looking at him.

"Your denial was amusing at first but now it's getting old," he responded.

"Shut up and look at all these books," I said as I glided across the rug to the first shelf. "This is insane."

"Like you?" Meri quipped.

I shot him a look over my shoulder, but nothing could distract me from what I'd found. The attic was huge, and I realized it was more like one big, open third story than a cramped storage space. There were rows and rows of bookshelves that stretched to the ceiling, and the other wall was lined with shelves all the way around the perimeter too.

Most of the books were just an extensive collection of fiction dating back to the first books made on a printing press. I didn't even want to think about how much they were worth. Some were just paperbacks and library copies, but there were a lot of first editions too. In the middle of everything was a shelf that looked different. The wood was different, and the books in that case looked like they were written in Latin. I wasn't sure because I couldn't read Latin, but it was definitely an old language.

"I wonder what these are?" I pondered out loud.

"Witch books," Meri answered.

"What?"

"Magic books."

I pulled one off the shelf. "How do I know you're telling the truth? I can't even read what they say."

"That one is The Book of Magical Charms," he said.

"Oh, really?" I asked and opened the book. "What is it about?"

"Your guess is as good as mine. As long as I've been alive, no witch has ever been powerful enough to decipher it."

"That's convenient," I said and put it back before pulling a black book from the shelf below. "What about this one?"

"That is a copy of the Malleus Maleficarum. The Hammer of Witches. It was a witch-hunting manual," Meri said.

"Then what is it doing here?"

"One of your ancestors stole it from the witch hunter who tried to kill her. She put a hex on his family, but only to end their witch hunting. As long as the book is in your possession, that bloodline will not hunt witches again."

"There are families of witches and witch hunters too?"

"Yes."

"I think I want to know more about some of these," I said.

"What do you want to know?" Meri asked.

Reminding myself that, for my grip on sanity, I should not be conversing with a talking black cat about witch books, I pulled my phone out of my pajama pocket and Googled for the closest antique book dealer. I expected to have to drive into the nearest city, but there was a place called Badersmith Books right in Coventry.

I grabbed a stack of the books that seemed like the most important ones and headed back to the bedroom to get dressed. Once I was presentable, I slipped the books into an old backpack from my college days and headed out to the car.

When I opened the door, Meri jumped in and made himself at home in the passenger seat. It wasn't the strangest thing to happen in my recent memory, so I decided to let him stay.

"If you're riding along, then you can at least give me directions to Badersmith Books," I said as I fastened my seatbelt.

I reasoned that it would prove that Meri wasn't real. If he was just my imagination, then he wouldn't be able to give me accurate directions to the bookstore because I'd never been there before. It might also mean that I was completely nuts, but at that point I wasn't sure which I was more afraid of. Was it worse to be crazy or to find out that everything I thought I knew about the world was wrong?

As I pulled into the small parking lot for Badersmith Books, I had to stifle a whimper. Meri's directions had been spot on.

"I just saw the directions when I looked the place up on my phone," I reasoned. "The cat didn't just give me directions. It was just imprinted on my subconscious mind. That has to be it. I'm not crazy and the cat doesn't talk."

"Brighton, calm down," Meri said.

I covered my ears with my hands and closed my eyes. "I'm not crazy and the cat doesn't talk."

If I hadn't still been seatbelted in, the tap on my driver's side window would have made me jump high enough to hit my head on the roof of my car. It was Sheriff Wilson, Thorn, and he was looking at me like I was a nutjob babbling to herself in her car at the bookstore. With her cat. Which I was.

He stepped back and I got out of the car. Without even thinking about it, I left the door open long enough for Meri to hop out too. When I saw him sitting on the ground next to me, I didn't say anything. There was no way I was going to leave an animal in the car while I went into the store. I'd seen all those PSAs about how cracking a window isn't enough. That cat had become the bane of my existence, but I wouldn't let him suffer.

"Why are you here, ma'am?" Thorn's voice was curt, and clearly he wasn't glad to see me.

"Brighton," I corrected. "You keep calling me ma'am and it makes me feel old or like a suspect."

"Should you be a suspect?" He cocked one eyebrow high.

I had to bite the inside of my cheek to keep from smiling because I found the gesture completely adorable. I found Thorn attractive and intriguing, but it was evident he found me to be a pain in the butt.

"No, I shouldn't be," I said and squared my shoulders. "But as far as what I'm doing here, it's a bookstore. I'm here about books."

"You need to wait here," Thorn said and he abruptly turned and walked into the store without so much as a backward glance.

That was until he got to the door. Before he pulled it open, he stood there for a moment studying me. His look had softened, and he regarded me with curiosity when I'd expected contempt. Before he ducked into the store, he held up his index finger indicating that I should wait a minute. I went around to the passenger side and removed the stack of books from my backpack.

I did wait one minute, and then annoyed at being made to wait in the parking lot of the bookstore with no explanation, I proceeded inside.

Once I was inside, I stayed near the door because I could hear Thorn and another man talking. I'd let the door close behind me softly, so my presence didn't interrupt their conversation.

I realized quite quickly that it was Thorn asking the man about a rumor he'd heard. Apparently, Ralph, the bookstore owner, and Harkin had a loud argument the week before at Mann's Gas & Grocery. Ralph admitted to the argument without missing a beat, but unfortunately for my curious heart, he didn't go into any detail as to what the argument was about. Thorn pressed the issue, but Ralph continued to insist it was a stupid squabble about the last box of cinnamon cereal.

After a few more attempts, Thorn grew increasingly frustrated and turned to leave. He didn't seem pleased to find me standing near the entrance as he made his way to the door.

I ignored his piercing stare and brushed past him to the counter where Ralph stood looking bored. After setting the books down, I introduced myself and told him where I found the books.

"Hello, I'm Brighton Longfield. I just moved into Hangman's House. I was going to clean out the attic, but to my surprise, I found that the attic is actually a fairly extensive home library. I brought some of the books that piqued my interest. I was hoping you could tell me more about them."

I could have sworn that he looked nervous. "Those are old spell books," he said with an anxious chuckle as his eyes darted behind me. "Of course, they're all nonsense."

When he kept staring over my shoulder, I turned to see Thorn standing in the spot I'd just vacated. He was watching us and listening to our conversation. I fought the urge to get annoyed because he was doing the exact same thing I'd just been doing. How could I fault him for that?

He must have been convinced that we were just discussing old books because he turned with a wave and left. As soon as he was out the door, Ralph came out from behind the counter. He went to the doors, locked them, and turned the sign in the window to closed before returning to me.

It unnerved me at first, and Ralph must have picked up on that. "I get nervous when there are books of this value just hanging around out in the open. I locked the door as a precaution."

That made sense, and I relaxed a little. But I tensed up again when he picked up one of the books and began caressing it in a way that was a little over-the-top creepy. I took a step back as I watched him flip through the books and stroke their pages and spines. It took all of my strength not to snatch them all away from him to protect their dignity. He was practically slobbering over the volumes.

The very last one he paged through had him shaking with excitement. He looked as though he was going to explode, and then he hugged the book to his chest and turned to me. It was a handwritten tome with a black leather cover that had been stamped with a gold pentagram. Of the books, I thought it would be the one of the least value, but I'd been wrong.

"I will give you two hundred and fifty thousand for this book right now," he said. "We'll call the bank on speakerphone if you like and they'll confirm for you that the check is real," he said, turning his body slightly away from me as if to keep me from taking the volume back.

Just then, Meri jumped on my shoulder again. "Do not sell your ancestral magic books, Brighton. No amount of money in the world is worth it."

My stomach churned at the thought of turning down that much money. Especially since it was for a book that up until an hour ago, I didn't even know I had. How could I miss something I'd never used or needed? Still, given the way Ralph was acting, I trusted that cat more than his creepy butt. I had to question my sanity, but it just felt like the right thing to do.

"No thanks," I said and reached over to pull the book from his clutches. "I'm not in the market to sell them right now."

His face turned red and his eyes narrowed. "Well, I'm busy man, and we're closing early today." Ralph came around the counter.

As I grabbed my books, he moved closer to me crowding me toward the door. "I'll just be going then," I said as I hugged the stack of books to my chest protectively. It was a mirror of what he'd done, but the difference was that they were my books.

He rushed me to the door, and I was more than happy to oblige. Ralph had left the key in the lock, so I twisted it and let myself out. When I looked back, he was glaring at me and relocking the door.

Meri was on my heels, and then we were back in the car and headed home. "If you knew what the books were, why didn't you just tell me?" I demanded from Meri once we were on the road. "Why did you make me go in there to get answers you already had?"

"Because now you believe me, and you wouldn't have if I didn't let Ralph do the convincing for me," he said and licked his paw casually.

"I don't know about that," I said. "Maybe the book is just worth a lot of money. But I would definitely have it appraised by a second source at least before taking an offer for it. He could have low-balled me. It could be worth twice that much."

"Brighton, you cannot sell that book," Meri said as we pulled into the driveway. "That's your family legacy, and it could cause catastrophic damage if it ever fell into the wrong hands."

I got out of the car and let Meri out. "Let's go inside and I promise to try and set some of my skepticism aside if you'll tell me more."

Once we were inside, I checked the cabinets and found a box of herbal tea that seemed familiar but that I didn't remember buying. It wasn't surprising as I often mindlessly threw things in my shopping basket.

When the tea was made, I settled in on the sofa in the living room with the books stacked next to me. It would have been nice to have a fire to make the room more cozy, but I was too worried about burning Hangman's House down to even attempt it.

While I sipped my tea, Meri jumped into my lap and made himself comfortable. "What do you want to know?"

"I want to know about my family. You say we're witches, but no one other than Maude has ever even mentioned anything about magic. My grandmother didn't want me moving here. Is this why? But that doesn't make any sense. Why would they have all turned away from their heritage?"

"The Tuttlesmiths and the Skeenbauers are the founding families of Coventry. If you go to the courthouse, there is a statue outside of the two original witch families. But it's not just a courthouse, Brighton, it's a temple, and they built it on a ley line. Do you know what that is?"

"It's some kind of magnetic line that circles the Earth," I answered.

"It's more than that, Brighton. It's a line of power, and it acts as a beacon to paranormal creatures and magic. Anyone who has any kind of magical ability will find it amplified when they stand on the node of a ley line. The courthouse is a temple built on a place of power.

"The Skeenbauers and Tuttlesmiths lived in harmony for a long time, but eventually, the human population began to grow. The two families disagreed on how to manage magic and what laws to enforce in Coventry. The Skeenbauers didn't want to allow humans to move into the town, but the Tuttlesmiths could see that times were changing. They knew there was no way to keep them out forever, and they felt it was better to hide in plain sight.

"The disagreement eventually led to feuding. It was never outwardly violent, but took the form of more subtle hexes like poisoning each other's crops and infertility spells. After decades of that, both families dwindled to only a few descendants.

"It would appear that the witch families had been lost to the modern era, but forty years ago, Amelda Skeenbauer became the matriarch and leader of the Skeenbauer coven. She renewed the feud in a grab for power, but it wasn't difficult. The Tuttlesmith numbers had dwindled even more than the Skeenbauers. There weren't many of them left at all, and most of them hadn't paid much attention to maintaining their powers. She was successful in driving them out of Coventry. The one witch who remained was powerful enough to oppose her, but Amelda turned to the humans and had her thrown into an asylum. It didn't take much to get a single woman committed back in those days.

"For Amelda the move was more about pride than it was about closing Coventry off to humans. By then, it was too impractical. But she and the other Skeenbauer witches had Coventry all to themselves. They had the temple and the ley line power under their complete control. Until you came along."

"How does anyone not notice this going on? How can magic hide in plain sight? We're in the internet age."

"Well, Coventry does draw a lot of parapsychologists because honestly, the proof that magic exists is right there out in the open. Most people are conditioned to ignore it, though. They write those who do believe off as nutjobs. The non-witch residents of Coventry never seem to notice the parapsychologists or the investigations. Humans willfully ignore it all."

"But if Maude was so powerful, why did she allow the humans to take her away? Why did she let them keep her locked up like that?"

"They kept her drugged and sedated for a long time, Brighton. By the time they stopped doing that, she had lost the will to use her powers. They dwindled to almost nothing once she left the radius of the node and stopped practicing. Plus, the way her family treated her broke her spirit. What Amelda did wasn't the worst. Maude suffered far worse at the hands of her own family. They disowned her and took all of her assets other than the deed to Hangman's House. They had the deed, but for some reason, they could never sell the house. No one would buy it. I believe that whatever magic Maude had left, she used it to ensure that this house would end up back in the hands of a worthy Tuttlesmith. She could never get away because she made sure you would end up here."

"I wish I would have tried harder to get her out," I said. "But I didn't know. I thought she was just crazy. I loved her, but the stories she told couldn't possibly have been true."

"Well, now you know that they are, and you can protect the Tuttlesmith legacy,"

Meri said and stretched out his front legs while flexing his impressive claws. "But you're going to need to learn to read Latin if you want to use most of those books."

"I don't want to use them," I said and shook my head. "I'm not a witch, and I have no power. I'm just crazy like Maude. You can't talk. None of this can be real."

"What about the blinds, Brighton?" Meri asked. "That's your doing. You're closing them magically. You may not have accepted it yet, but your subconscious is using your powers to protect you."

"No, I'm just doing it in my sleep," I said.

"There's a way to prove it," Meri said.

"How?"

"You can set up a camera tonight when you go to sleep."

It was completely bonkers, but that night I did set my phone up to record the window while I slept. I knew it would prove once and for all that I was shutting them while sleepwalking, I was completely losing my mind, and that I needed to book an appointment with a mental healthcare professional sooner rather than later.

Chapter Six

As soon as I woke up the next morning, I watched the video. My jaw was slack as I watched the blinds close around two in the morning. I rewound and watched the video three more times. The blinds definitely closed, and there was no one closing them.

That was the moment that I began to believe that maybe Maude wasn't crazy after all, but I wasn't quite at a place where I could admit it. I decided the best thing to do was to call my mom and ask her what she knew. The phone rang a few times and went to voicemail. I set my phone down on the bed and was about to try and move on with my day when it rang again.

"Hello, darling," my mother sang into the phone. "I'd begun to think I was never going to hear from you again. I'm glad to hear you're alive."

"Hi, Mom. Sorry it took me so long to call. Things got a little dark in my head after Donnie and I divorced, and everything just sort of spiraled out of control. I should have called."

"No worries now, Brighton. I'm just happy to hear from you."

"I wanted to ask you about something," I said.

"Go ahead."

"Well, is there anything about our family that I should know? I mean, are there any weird things about us?"

"Oh, lord, Brighton. I have no idea what you're talking about, but I think there are weird things about every family."

"No, I mean, like anything... I don't know how to put this... Like, maybe paranormal."

"You should be careful talking about that stuff, Brighton. You know my Aunt Maude was crazy, and I'd hate for you to end up like her. You said your head went somewhere dark. Maybe you need to see someone. Do you know anyone who could recommend a good therapist?"

"I don't think that's what I need, but you're right." I didn't think she was right, but if she didn't know anything about the magic and witches, I didn't want her to start thinking I really was crazy. "How have you been, Mom?"

After that we just chatted for a while until she had to go for her vitamin infusion appointment. I wasn't quite sure what that was, but it sounded an awful lot like getting an IV full of vitamins.

Once I was off the phone with her, I had to figure out who else I could ask. I remembered that my grandma had warned me not to come to Coventry, so I decided to call her.

"Hello, darling," my grandmother sang into the phone. "I just got a text message from your mother letting me know that you're not dead after all."

"Sorry I haven't called in a while, Grams."

"It's okay, I'm just glad to speak to you now, but please don't be a stranger in the future."

"I won't," I said. "But I do need to ask you about something important."

"Anything, Brighton."

"Why did you tell me not to move to Coventry?"

"Oh, my. Brighton, did you move into Hangman's House?"

"I did."

"And have you met Meri yet?" she asked.

"I have."

"I worked so hard to keep your mother out of all of this. Which is why she couldn't tell you anything when you called, right?"

"She couldn't."

"But you know that Maude wasn't crazy now, don't you?"

"Either she's not crazy or I'm nuts too."

"First off, I want to say that no matter what that blasted cat tells you, we did what we did to protect Maude. We weren't trying to hurt her or take advantage of her. If we hadn't dispensed of her assets, that asylum she lived in was going to take it all. We didn't keep the money, Brighton. We donated it all to families in need. The second thing I need to tell you is that you need to move out of Hangman's House and leave Coventry for good. Amelda Skeenbauer is not going to take it well that a Tuttlesmith witch has moved back into town, and I'm afraid you probably aren't strong enough to deal with her. Brighton, the safest thing for you to do is leave. You can come stay with me if you need a place to live. I promise I'll give you your space."

"I'll think about it, Grandma. I really will," I said. "Hey, do you know who around here could teach me Latin?"

She let out a huge sigh. "You're going to do the exact opposite of what I've suggested. I can feel it, but if you really want to learn Latin, then there are archives at the records department in Coventry. I'd guess that whomever is running it these days can help you."

"The records department?"

"At the courthouse."

"Thank you, Grandma," I said.

"Call me if you need me. Or you know, just call me sometimes."

"I will."

"Be safe, Brighton."

"I will."

When I was off the phone, I scooped up the handwritten book and started to head out. Meri interrupted me.

"Hey, grab a big handbag so that I can come with you," he said. "You can sneak me into the courthouse."

I went upstairs and grabbed a big tote bag from my closet and put it on the floor so that Meri could jump in. At that point, I'd barely registered it as crazy that I was smuggling my talking cat into the ancient temple that served as a courthouse to have someone help me translate my family book of magic.

There was a sign hanging inside the courthouse that told visitors what was located on each floor. The sign said that the archives were in the basement.

I took the elevator down and stepped off into a large room that seemed to go on for miles. It was strange because it seemed like the basement had to be bigger than the actual courthouse above it. I wondered how many of the residents of Coventry knew that there was a catacomb of records under their feet.

"Can I help you?" The voice came from a desk located in the middle of the room beyond the first rows of shelves.

"Um, yes," I said and hurried toward the desk. "I was told that you might be able to help me with this book."

"Let me take a look at it," the man said as I slid the book gently across the counter to him. "My name is Remy. It's nice to meet you."

Remy's cheeks colored pink when he introduced himself to me, and it became obvious that he was quite shy. My guess was that was why he held the job in the basement courthouse records room. He probably didn't get many visitors.

I'd have put Remy in his thirties, but he could have been older or younger. He had a face that made it hard to tell. His skin was smooth like that of a younger person. But his eyes were a deep chocolate brown and they had a soulful look that made it obvious he'd seen some things in his lifetime. He was thin but I wouldn't say scrawny and definitely at least a head or two taller than me, but that wasn't saying much as I was quite short. So average height and appearance, but there was something else under the surface. Remy seemed unassuming, but I wasn't going to underestimate him just yet.

I watched as he looked over the book for a few moments. "We should go sit down," he said as he closed it and looked up at me.

"Sure," I said. "Lead the way. Oh, and I'm Brighton, by the way. It's nice to meet you as well."

He turned quickly and began walking toward a table on the other side of the desk, but I could swear I caught another blush. He was endearing for sure, and I felt completely relaxed and comfortable in his presence. A little niggling at the back of my brain made me wonder if the whole thing was a spell.

"You'd like my help interpreting the book?" Remy asked when were both seated.

"I would. I don't read Latin."

"This book isn't written in Latin," he said more confidently than anything else he'd said.

"It isn't?" My shoulders slumped. I'd been so close. "What language is it?"

"That's hard to say. Not because I don't know but because it's hard to describe. But don't worry, Brighton. I can read it."

"Can you tell me what's in it?" I asked.

"Well, it looks like a lot of what I guess are spells, incantations, and rituals. There might even be a few hexes and conjurings in there," he said it all so matter-of-factly as if there was nothing strange about me presenting him an old handwritten book of magic. "It's the Tuttlesmith family Grimoire. That means book of shadows or book of magic."

"Can you help me learn to read it?"

"I can..." Remy said before a pause. "But we'll need to keep it quiet and you need to keep that book hidden."

"Why?"

"Because some of the members of my family would do unkind things to get it. Plus, even to regular humans, it's probably worth a small fortune."

"You're a Skeenbauer?"

"Remy Skeenbauer at your service, but please don't worry, Brighton. Not all of us care about the silly feud. Including my amazing cousin," he said and stood up. "Hello, Annika."

I turned around and Annika was stepping off the elevator. She looked a little shocked to see me.

"Hey, Remy," she said with a smile. "Hello, Brighton," she said with a half frown that matched the cool tone of her voice.

I couldn't figure out why she was upset with me, and then I remembered. I'd completely forgotten about our lunch date.

"Oh my gosh," I said, standing up. "I'm so sorry, Annika. I totally flaked on our lunch date yesterday. I am the worst, and I know it. Please forgive me. I do want to have lunch with you. It's just that the shock of finding Harkin's body kind of left me stupid yesterday."

"I'll forgive you for forgetting me yesterday if you'll come to Dumbledore's with Remy and I for lunch today. We really need the details on Harkin's demise," she said with a slightly wicked glint in her eye.

"It's okay," Remy said. "You guys don't have to let me tag along." He blushed again. "We can go another time, Annika."

"Nonsense, Remy. We want you to come along, and you have to eat," Annika said before turning to me. "You don't mind if my favorite cousin comes along with us, do you?"

"Not at all," I said. "Remy, do you think it would be okay for me to take the book with us? Or do you have a safe you can store it in for me?"

"I will definitely lock it in my personal vault for you, Brighton."

"Thank you."

"Are you sure Dumbledore's is okay?" Annika asked while Remy was stowing my book. "I just realized that you might have bad memories about the place."

"No, it's fine," I said. "I think a stack of pancakes is just what I need."

The crowd at Dumbledore's diner was thinner at lunch than at dinner, but not by much. The place was still mostly full, but we didn't have to wait too long for a table.

Once Keisha had taken our orders, Annika thought that we should share our knowledge of Harkin's death and discuss our suspects. I looked around, and despite the crowd, no one was really paying attention to us. So I started.

"Well, I went to Badersmith books the other day, and I heard Thorn asking Ralph about a fight they had at Mann's," I said. "Oh, and I saw Harkin reject Prue at her store. He was so condescending and insulting to her. I mean, if he'd talked to me that way, I'd probably want to hurt him to."

"I don't know what she saw in that guy," Annika said. "But she really was sweet on him. I've heard the rumors of how nasty he was to her. Okay, so what I know is that Thorn was in Ruby's garden this morning nosing around. Ruby stood by watching him with papers in her hand. She looked furious."

"Who is Ruby?" I asked.

"She owns Ruby Red's Apothecary. She sells herbal soaps, shampoos, candles, and remedies to the normals, but Ruby supplies the rest of us with herbs for our spells," Annika dropped her voice to barely above a whisper for the last part.

"I don't understand why Ruby would be involved," Remy said.

"Because Harkin was killed with ricin," Keisha said as she set our plates down on the table. She'd approached while Remy was pondering Ruby's involvement. "At least that's what I heard from one of the deputies this morning."

"Oh." A lightbulb must have gone off in Remy's brain. "Ricin comes from castor beans."

"Yeah, and Ruby makes her own castor oil. I've bought some from her before for spells," Annika said and quickly recovered in front of Keisha. "I mean for dizzy spells."

After lunch, Remy and I went back to the records office. I'd left my bag behind so that Meri could get out and move around while we were gone.

Remy retrieved my book from his office, and he attempted to teach me some of the language in the book. He was sweet and patient the entire time, but I didn't think I was ever going to get it. I struggled enough with Spanish in school let alone a secret witch language that only a handful of people in the world understood.

"I'm never going to get this," I said with a huge, and even in my opinion, overly dramatic sigh.

"I can help you," Remy said with a nervous chuckle.

"I know you're trying so hard, but I don't think I'll get it even under your expert tutelage. I really do appreciate this, though."

"No, Brighton. I mean I can help you learn faster if you want. I have a way."

"Of course, I would love that..."

But I wasn't prepared for it when he began to chant in the language. His words were hypnotic and rolled off his tongue in waves that snaked into my brain. My head spun, and for a minute, it ached so badly that tears threatened to spill down my cheeks.

But just as quickly as it had begun, the pain and fog cleared. When I looked down at the book again, I could read it just as plainly as if it were written in English.

My heart began to pound out of my chest. What had he done to me? I grabbed the book and my bag and ran to the elevator. Thankfully, Meri had snuggled back into the tote bag for a nap at some point, so I had him with me.

The elevator chimed and the doors opened. I tried to dart inside, but I ran right into the wall of muscle that was Sheriff Thorn Wilson.

"Hello, Brighton," he said and tipped his hat to me.

"Hi, Sheriff," I said, and in my flustered state, I blurted out: "Is Ruby a suspect in Harkin's death?"

"Man, sometimes I hate small town gossip," he said. "That isn't any of your business. Maybe you should learn how to walk," Thorn said brusquely before stepping around me and walking toward Remy's desk.

I got entirely more satisfaction than I should have when I stuck my tongue out at Thorn's back as he walked away. Remy sort of smiled when he saw me do it, but when I caught him looking at me, his face fell. I couldn't tell if his expression was sad, uncertain, or a combination of both.

Instead of getting on the elevator, I waited. Thorn requested some document that Remy retrieved for him quickly. As the sheriff approached the elevator again, he gave me a stern look.

"If you're hanging around to ask Remy about these papers, don't bother. He's a good man and won't betray his duty to the town just to fuel your need for gossip."

"But…" I tried to defend myself, but Thorn stepped on the elevator and left me standing there.

Remy stood at the desk watching me again. He looked like he had something he wanted to say, but I knew that he was far too shy to approach me. He must have cast a spell on me to help me read the book, and I felt like I'd overreacted. I just wasn't used to all of the magic business, but there was something to it.

I walked back to the desk, and he relaxed a little. "I'm sorry that I freaked out. You just caught me off guard, but I do appreciate what you did. Will you help me learn more of the secrets in the book?"

"I will help you when you need it, Brighton, but I think your familiar would be a bigger help with that."

"My familiar?" I looked down at my purse and realized that Meri's ears were sticking out. "Oh, right," I said. "He, uh… Meri wanted to come along, so I let him."

"It's okay. I don't mind Meri at all. Like I said before, not all of us care about my grandmother's feud. That's her deal, not mine."

"Thank you so much for your help," I said. "And thank you for having lunch with us. It's nice to get to know people from town."

"Anytime, Brighton," Remy said, and I noticed that the pink color returned to his cheeks. "Come back anytime you need help or just want to shoot the breeze."

"You got it," I said.

It was strange, I almost felt like I wanted to give him a hug. Instead I settled for an awkward high-five and another round of nervous chuckles from both of us.

When I got back home, I put the frozen pizza that Meri and I had picked up from Mann's on the way home in the freezer and sat down at the kitchen table to read the book some more.

Meri and I spent the rest of the afternoon and evening reading the book and eating pizza. Well, I read, and he napped next to me. I didn't dare say any of the words in the book out loud and resisted the urge to gather the materials listed for the spells. I'd seen that movie *The Mummy*. I wasn't about to mess around with the powers in the book.

Chapter Seven

A sound roused me from my sleep, but I didn't quite catch what it was. When I looked at my phone, I saw that it was three in the morning. I'd heard somewhere that was some sort of paranormal hour, but I'd never had reason to believe it before.

I heard the sound again, and that time I did identify it. The scratching noise was coming from out in the hallway just outside of where I could see out the door. At first, I thought it was just Meri sharpening his claws on the wood floor.

"Meri, knock it off," I said and rubbed my eyes.

"Huh? Knock what off?" he said and sat up.

It wasn't the cat in the hallway because Meri was curled up next to me in his usual spot. Without thinking about it, I put my hand on his back for reassurance. When the scratching noise came again, I felt the hair on the back of his haunches stand up.

"That's not good," he said quietly.

"I don't suppose it's just a rogue squirrel," I said with a nervous laugh.

"No, Brighton. Scratching like that comes from one source. It's a spirit and it's not good."

"Like an angry ghost?" I whispered.

"Either that or a demon."

"So I guess that means demons are real too."

"They are, but there's still a chance it's just an angry spirit instead or perhaps a trickster. Either way, I'm not sure how it got in here. This house is heavily protected. That means that either there's a hole in the house's defenses, or that thing in the hallway is stronger that your family's magic."

"Awesome," I said. "What do we do?"

"Well, normally, I'd tell you to cast a protection spell, but the way your magical practice has been going, I think you'd actually summon a demon or perhaps steer an asteroid toward earth. Maybe we should just go in the hall and look," Meri said and stood up.

"Wait, what? You're going to go out there?"

"Or we can sit here and wait for it to come get us," Meri said as he stretched.

We both jumped when we heard the loud thump from the hallway. It was followed by the sound of footsteps running toward the spare bedroom on the other side, and then that bedroom door slammed.

"I should call the police," I said and reached for my phone. "That sounded like it might have actually been an intruder."

I slid out of the bed and closed the bedroom door as quickly and quietly as I could. Oddly enough, there was a deadbolt that I hadn't noticed before. I tried to lock it, but it just twisted impotently.

"We could hide in the closet."

Just as I said it, someone began to pound on the bedroom door. I swear that I almost peed my pants. Meri and I looked at each other and bolted for the closet.

Somehow, I managed to drop my phone on the way to our hiding spot. I wanted to go back out and get it, but every time I reached for the closet door handle, whoever or whatever was out there would unleash another volley of knocks on the bedroom door.

"They're not coming in," I finally said. "The bedroom door isn't locked or anything, but they're not coming in."

"We should go look," Meri said. "I just have a feeling. I think I can protect us. This has gone far enough."

"Okay," I said nervously.

I stood up and exited the closet. Another round of knocks sounded on the other side of the bedroom door, but I forced myself to keep moving toward it.

I put my hand on the knob and immediately noticed that it was ice cold. When I breathed out, my breath misted as the temperature in the room dropped down to freezing.

"Enough," I said and Meri and I both nodded our heads yes.

I threw the door open, and no one was there. At least, no one was right outside the door. I saw the specter of a woman in a white dress drift down the stairs. I ran out to the landing and watched as she floated into the living room and then disappeared.

"Let's go back to bed," Meri said.

"We're just going to go back to bed?"

"What else are we going to do? She seems to be done with whatever she was trying to do, and I'm tired. It's best if we try and ignore them as much as possible."

"Just ignore the ghosts?"

"Just ignore the ghosts," Meri confirmed, and we went back to bed.

The next morning, I woke up with a burning hunger for more knowledge about my family and our magic. I figured the best place to start was the Coventry Library. If the town was truly supernatural in origin, there had to be book there that could shed some light on the magic business I'd stumbled into. The early morning's run-in with a ghost had almost been forgotten. In the light of day, it sort of felt like a distant memory of a bad dream. So I decided to do what Meri had suggested and ignore it. I'd focus my efforts on researching witchcraft.

I'd thought to check the internet, but I knew it would be too hard to tell what was real information and what was just made-up junk to attract clicks.

I had the sense that there had to be a section of magic books at the library, and I wasn't going to get my hands on them unless I went there. I could nose around and find out where they were kept. If the Tuttlesmith family really did help found the city of Coventry, then I reasoned that I had a right to any books they'd helped procure for the library.

Breakfast was leftover potatoes for me and a bowl of beef for Meri. He wanted to come along, but I said that I needed to feel out the situation before I brought him into the library in a tote bag. I'd gotten away with it when it came to Remy, but I worried the library would be a different story.

The library was across from the courthouse. I parked my car on the street and crossed to the stone steps that led to the entrance. The place was huge, but it didn't give that impression at first. I wondered if that was a spell. The thought came to me that it was a spell to keep the humans from thinking too much about the parts of the library they couldn't access.

Inside, I could see that the library was split into two sections. Off to one side was busy with people browsing books and reading quietly in chairs.

The other side said Halls of the Mystic, and there was no one in there. That sounded like the place I needed to be, so I started to go through the massive arch that marked the barrier between the entryway and the magic wing of the library.

"Excuse me," a shrill voice rang out in the quiet library, and I turned to see an older woman hurrying toward me.

Despite the volume at which she'd called out to me, no one seemed to notice. "Excuse me," she called again in a harsher tone.

The woman was in her seventies and garbed in an ankle-length black dress with a purple smock on top. She had her gray hair pulled up in a severe bun at the back of her head that only served to accentuate her scowl.

"You can't go in there. Can't you read? That wing is closed for construction," she said and then tutted at me like I was soft in the head.

"Read what?" I said. "This wing doesn't look like it's under construction. If it is, you should really put up a sign."

"You can't see the sign?" she asked.

"What sign? No, I don't see a sign," I said with a disbelieving shake of my head. Was this woman completely nuts?

"Who are you?" She narrowed her eyes at me further.

"I'm Brighton Longfield. I just moved into my great-aunt's house. I live in Hangman's House. Anyway, I wanted to do some research, and this looks like exactly what I need," I said.

"Well, Ms. Longfield, I'm Amelda Skeenbauer. I'm the head librarian around here and also head of the Skeenbauer family. I suppose you know that your kind isn't welcome here. The Tuttlesmiths aren't welcome in Coventry. You should leave this library and Coventry before you force my hand." She practically spit at me.

"Force your hand at what?" I asked, but I really didn't want to know. "Besides, I don't have anywhere else to go. Hangman's House is my home, and I intend to stay." I squared my shoulders and defiantly maintained eye contact despite Amelda's obvious attempt to stare me down.

Amelda raised her hands up in front of her chest and curled her fingers into what looked like an imitation of claws. She began to chant something under her breath that I couldn't quite understand, but I got the distinct feeling that I was about to be zapped, hexed, or cursed.

"Grannie, knock it off."

I looked over Amelda's shoulder and found Annika approaching us. She must have come in while Amelda was scolding me, and I hadn't noticed because I'd been so focused on the fact that the witch was about to spell me with something unpleasant.

Amelda's hands went to her side, and her previously menacing demeanor melted somewhat. "It's good to see you, Annika," she said with a smile. "What brings you to the library today?"

"I'm not sure. I just had a feeling that I was needed here, and it looks like my intuition was right. You should stop being so mean to my new friend," Annika said as she wrapped one arm around her grandmother and then bent to give her a kiss on the temple. "Play nice."

"You can't be friends with this...." Amelda bit back a curse when Annika shot her a reproving look. "You can't be friends with a Tuttlesmith. It's just not right."

"I love you, Grannie," Annika said before coming over to me.

She linked her arm through mine and led me toward the Halls of the Mystic. "Thank you," I said as we walked under the arch.

"Annika," Amelda called out to us. The first part of the word "Ann" was quite stern, but her voice had deflated by the time she got to the "ika" part. "I love you too."

Annika and I took a seat at one of the huge mahogany tables in the magical research section. "You know, I don't really pay much attention to all this magical stuff. It's so important to my Grannie, but I could take it or leave it. But I can probably help you with enough of it to keep you out of trouble."

"Out of trouble?"

"Yeah, like the Rule of Three," Annika said. "That's something you have to know."

"What is the Rule of Three?"

"The Rule of Three states that whatever you put out into this world, you get back times three. So if you do good, you get good back in a measure of three times what you put into the world. But if you do mean or harmful things, you also get those back times three," she said. "Oh, but you can't do good just to get good back times three, Brighton. That's another one of the most important things. You cannot use any powers you have for personal gain. Magic is about nature and nature is about balance, so you can't use it for personal gain and upset the balance."

"What about black and white magic?" I asked. "That's what they talk about in the movies."

"Okay, so that definitely exists, but there are other types as well. Like, there's green magic, for example. Those are the witches that can heal someone by naming a plant after the sick person and then tending to it. They can grow the most delicious strawberries by fertilizing the soil with love and kindness from their heart. They're basically nature fairies, but witches. Oh, and there are kitchen witches. They can weave magic into their cuisine. Some of them don't even know they're witches. People just see them as extremely talented cooks."

"But black magic does exist?"

"It does," Annika said with a shrug. "But the rule of three keeps it in check. Most people aren't willing to pay the price to use it. Sometimes they do. Sometimes they have to, but most people avoid it whenever they can."

"So it's not just evil witches that use black magic?"

"Nope. I mean, a lot of black magic is evil, Brighton. Most of it is. But some of it has to do with communicating with the dead. And there are ways and reasons to use it that aren't inherently evil. It's a gray area for sure. But that's because nature is a gray area. Gaia, that's Mother Earth or Mother Nature, is both loving and cruel."

"So how do I…" I wasn't even sure how or what to ask.

"How do you know what is okay and what isn't?" Annika asked. "Well, the golden rule for witches is this: And it harm none, do what thou wilt."

"So as long as you're not hurting anyone, it's okay," I asked.

"Yep. It's pretty simple, huh? Well, I mean it can become complicated if you want it to. Like some witches believe that animals are a gift from the goddess to use and they eat meat. Some see animals as falling under the protection of the golden rule, and they don't eat or use any animal products. So, vegans. And then there are the ones who believe that plants fall under that protection too. They try to live off the energy of the sun or something. Goddess bless them, they don't last very long. They try, though. But it doesn't have to be complicated for you, Brighton. Your heart will tell you what's right for you. My intuition told me to come here today, so I did. If you're not used to listening to your intuition, then it's time to start."

"This is a lot," I said.

"It is probably pretty overwhelming, but you can always ask me if you need help. You've got Meri too. I assume that he's made his introductions?"

"He has."

"See, you're going to be fine. I can feel it," she said with a wink. "But unless you've got more questions right now, I should probably get back to my shop. Fashion waits for no one. Oh, and someone boosted a rare amethyst and tiger's eye necklace from the store. It was worth a ton, but my insurance company said they're going to give me a hundred bucks. So I've got to call them and yell at my claims adjuster."

As Annika and I walked out of the library, we ran into Ruby and another library patron talking on the front steps. I'd never met Ruby, but she and Annika exchanged hellos before Ruby launched back into giving the other woman an earful about "the nerve of that Sheriff Wilson for questioning me. I can't believe he would accuse me of poisoning that Harkin jerk just because some of my castor beans are missing."

I couldn't help but interrupt. "How do you know that some of your castor beans are missing?"

"I keep my garden in pristine order. It is as neat and tidy as can be, but someone trampled my hemlock to get to the castor beans. They were also sloppy when they cut them off. I always make precise cuts. These beans were hacked off with... I don't know. The savage probably cut them with dull scissors or something else equally as outrageous."

Ruby didn't ask me why I wanted to know. She just turned back to her companion and began her conversation again. I got out of there before Ruby could ask me why I wanted to know about her castor beans. It was a good thing too, because I wasn't even sure why I wanted to know just yet.

Chapter Eight

A few days later, I was still trying to settle into life in Coventry and come to terms with the fact that I was a was a witch from a formerly powerful coven.

I hadn't left the house much, but instead Meri had been trying to teach me the basics of magic. It turned out that doing magic wrong can be a disaster. Fortunately, Meri had been able to fix it when I almost burnt Hangman's House down, busted a pipe in the kitchen, and nearly set a swarm of locusts on the neighbors.

So we'd stripped it down to the bare bones. He tried to teach me to feel my magic. "I think you'll get a better idea if you go to the courthouse. It's on the ley line, and you should be able to feel that. You just go there and stand on the node."

"And then what?" I asked. "I've been to the courthouse before. I didn't feel anything."

"You've got to open yourself up to it. The statue out front is exactly on the node. Go stand in the circle the figures created. Close your eyes and open yourself up."

"I have no idea how to do that," I said.

"Just try it," Meri huffed. "Please. If it doesn't work, I'll think of something else."

With those instructions in mind, I got in my car and drove to the town square. Car parked and mind as open as possible, I made my way to the witch statue in front of the courthouse.

While I stood there with my eyes closed trying to feel the power flowing through the ley line node, I began to try and come up with a spell to help. I knew that magic could cause huge problems if it was used incorrectly, but I figured a little chant about being open and receiving the universe's energy couldn't hurt. Unfortunately, I couldn't come up with anything that rhymed.

Also, I forgot that I was in public. I was standing there with my eyes closed trying to whisper a spell that wouldn't cause an explosion or a plague, when someone tapped me on the shoulder.

I jumped half out of my skin, and when I opened my eyes, Sheriff Thorn Wilson stood there looking a cross between amused and concerned. It was sort of the way people look at zoo animals when they are behaving strangely.

"Is it true that you had a crazy great-aunt that used to live in Coventry?" he asked.

"I did. My Great-Aunt Maude spent most of her life in an institution."

I answered him quickly before I realized that he was implying that I was crazy too. Before I could think of a brilliant response or get myself arrested for assaulting a police officer, Thorn just shook his head and started to walk away.

It didn't matter how handsome he was or how much his blue eyes sparkled in the afternoon sun, he didn't get to make those kinds of insinuations. I went after him, and that time, I tapped him on the shoulder.

He turned around to look at me, and his gorgeous blue eyes suddenly seemed stormy. "What is it?"

"Maude may have been crazy, but she was a good loving woman. The world was a better place with her in it, and her passing was a loss. You should learn some manners. You've got this whole Deputy-Do-Right persona going on, but you're secretly just a jerk."

He opened his mouth to say something, but then just made a *humph* sound and walked off again. A couple of times, I thought he was going to stop and come back, but he didn't. It was probably better that way as I doubted I'd endeared him to my cause.

The worst part was that even though he'd all but accused me of being crazy, I found myself even more attracted to him. It was an inconvenient and unwelcome revelation, but I pushed it out of my mind when I saw Cassidy across the square pawing through the grass on the library lawn. I walked quickly over to where she was crying and searching.

"What's wrong, Cassidy?" I asked as I dropped to my knees next to her. "What happened?"

"I dropped Hattie's grocery money." She sniffled. "She won't use her debit card or write a check. I have to go to the bank once a week to get money for groceries. I lost it. She's going to be so angry." Cassidy moaned the last part.

"Well, let's keep looking. I know we can find it. Are you sure this is where you dropped it?"

"I've looked everywhere else between the bank and here. If it's not here, then I dropped it before and someone has already taken the money." She sniffled again. "Hattie is going to be livid. I'll probably be fired."

"No, we'll find it," I said and stood up.

I walked around the square looking in the grass for the lost cash. When I was turned away from the courthouse for a moment, a prickly sensation crept up my spine. It was as if I could feel someone watching me with the same disdain I'd gotten from Amelda, but she was in the library.

I should have just shaken the feeling off, but instead I turned around to look at the courthouse. In the far right window on the top floor was what looked like a pale figure starting down at me. The sight wouldn't have been that alarming except that, from what I could see at the distance, the figure had black holes for eyes, and when it opened its mouth, that appeared to be a midnight black chasm as well.

Before I could get Cassidy's attention to look, she called out, "I found it!"

I turned around to find her waving the money in the air and smiling like a kid on Christmas morning. When I looked back at the window, the figure was gone. I decided to write it off as my overactive imagination.

"Hey," Cassidy said as she tucked the money into her purse and dramatically closed the zipper. "I didn't notice those purple streaks in your hair before."

I pulled a handful of my hair in front of my face, and sure enough, streaks of violet, lavender, and eggplant ran through it like highlights. "Oh, this, yeah... I thought I'd try something different. You must not have seen it before because you were too busy looking for the money. Or the light wasn't hitting it right. New town, new me," I said with a smile.

"I think it's awesome," Cassidy said. "Thanks for helping me look. I gotta go or Hattie is going to have kittens. She hates when it takes me too long at the bank. I swear the old broad constantly thinks I'm going to steal from her. Which I would never do. Anyway, bye."

Chapter Nine

I pulled an elastic from my purse and tied my hair back in the hopes that would make the new purple coloring less noticeable. If people hadn't already decided that the new girl in town was a bit off, the purple hair was going to do it for them for sure.

My next stop was Mann's for some groceries and supplies. I needed to get some smoked salmon for Meri since he'd insisted that familiars did not eat canned cat food. It was a good thing I'd found that money in the jar on the top shelf of the cupboard, and part of me kind of hoped that Maude had hidden some more around the house, because it wasn't like I could do a spell to bring in money or even a job. So far, any spells I'd cast with good intentions had backfired spectacularly, I couldn't imagine what would happen if I tried to cast one for personal gain.

I needed some food too, and I'd decided to add some broccoli to my potatoes.

Since I had to buy Meri his expensive smoked salmon, frozen broccoli was my best option.

In the frozen food aisle, I ran into Cassidy and Hattie. Cassidy was getting some frozen tater tots from one of the cases while Hattie stood by the cart.

I didn't meant to brush past them, but Hattie had the cart in the middle of the aisle. When I did, the edge of Hattie's cart knocked my book out of the back pocket of my purse. I'd forgotten that I'd wedged it in there earlier. It hit the cart and then fell to the floor.

Hattie and I both dove for it, but she managed to snag it first. "Tuttlesmith Coven Book of Shadows." She mused softly after glancing at the cover. "Cassidy, hurry up, girl. I'm getting another of my migraines. I want to leave now," she barked at Cassidy as she handed the book back to me.

Something about that whole scene didn't sit right with me, but I had no idea what was wrong. I just knew that something was wrong. My intuition had kicked in, and as Annika suggested, I was trying to listen to it.

Before I could ponder it too much more, the woman checking out in the lane next to mine bent over to pick up one of her bags. When she did, the collar of her crisp, white shirt fell open just enough for me to see that she wore a beautiful retro amethyst and tiger's eye necklace. Her hand flitted to her collar as soon as it happened and concealed the necklace. The whole thing happened so fast that I wasn't sure I'd even really seen it.

I thought about calling Annika right then, but I didn't know who the woman was. She was a statuesque blonde in what looked like expensive clothes. When I went out in the parking lot to leave, the woman was getting into a top-of-the-line Mercedes. She obviously had money to buy whatever she wanted, so I couldn't help but doubt that she was Annika's shoplifter. The last thing I wanted to do was cause more trouble in town.

After dinner, I lay in bed and studied the book until I couldn't keep my eyes open anymore. I put it in the nightstand drawer and clicked off the lamp before settling under the covers.

What felt like seconds later, but was actually the middle of the night, my eyes flicked open with a start. I could feel that there was someone in the room with me. My first thought was that it was Ralph. He'd wanted the book bad enough to break into my house to steal it.

I rolled over on my back to try and rouse Meri from his sleep when I heard an icy whisper in my ear. Suddenly, I was completely paralyzed with my eyes open staring at the ceiling.

The sound of the nightstand drawer opening and the rustling of pages was followed by a loud shriek from Meri. From what I could tell, he'd pounced on the intruder from his hiding spot. I heard a scuffle, and then a feminine voice that sounded vaguely familiar cried out.

Someone ran out of the room and down the stairs.

Meri jumped onto my chest. "Snap out of it, Brighton. You're not paralyzed, you've been tricked into thinking you were."

And then I could move again. I first checked for the book which was lying on the floor undamaged.

"Meri, did you see who it was? Do you know who broke in?"

"No, but..." He sneezed. "They certainly smelled like lavender and baby powder."

"I know that smell," I said and picked up my phone to call the sheriff's office. "I definitely know that smell."

Chapter Ten

A sleepy-looking Thorn showed up about twenty minutes later to take a report about the break-in. I found a tin of coffee in the cabinet that somehow wasn't stale and brewed a pot while he looked around the outside of the house.

When he came back into the house, he walked around downstairs and upstairs before finding me in the kitchen. The knob for the back door was broken, but I could swear that Thorn rolled his eyes when I suggested that Hattie had done it. Perhaps it was because he was tired, but I thought it was possible I'd imagined it too.

"I think it was Hattie Driggs that broke in," I said.

"There's no way it was her, Brighton," he said without looking at me. "Hattie is blind, and there's no way she could have done this."

"The cat... I mean... What I'm trying to say is that I smelled the scent that lingers around Hattie."

"What scent would that be?" he asked with one eyebrow cocked.

"She smells like lavender and baby powder," I said and handed him a cup of coffee.

"Brighton, seriously? Do you know how many people probably smell like baby powder and lavender? That's hardly evidence," he said. "I know this was scary, but you can't just accuse elderly blind women of breaking into your home because you're freaked out. That's not how we do things around here."

"She's not blind," I said indignantly. "She read the title of a book I dropped at the store this afternoon."

"You're mistaken," he said with a sigh. "You need to get in touch with the town locksmith tomorrow and beef up the house's security. These old locks are just asking for trouble." He drained his cup of coffee in a couple of gulps and set the cup down on the counter. "Thank you for the coffee. I'll see myself out."

When I was sure he was gone, I asked Meri: "Are you sure it was lavender and baby powder you smelled?"

"Don't let Officer Hunky get to you, Brighton. Of course that's what I smelled."

"Well, then, I'm going to have to confront Hattie," I said and planted my hands on my hips. "I can just intimidate her into confessing. How hard can it be?"

"That's a bad idea, Brighton. People in this town think she's a sweet old lady. Officer Hunky will end up arresting you for threatening her or something. It would be better if you wait until she's out and sneak into her house. You can find some kind of proof. Then, they'll have to believe you."

"Oh, so burglary is fine but confronting her isn't?" I asked.

"Yeah, just don't get caught."

Chapter Eleven

Two days later, my opportunity to snoop presented itself. Meri had been keeping an eye on Hattie's place, so when Cassidy left to run errands, and Hattie slipped out a while later, Meri came to tell me it was time.

I found a key to the back door inside a fake plastic rock on the back porch. It wasn't a very good hiding spot as the rock didn't look real at all, and I wondered if she'd made the mistake because she was blind or because she was cheap.

Once inside, I quickly found her office on the second floor. Her important papers were in a file drawer in her desk, and her declaration of benefits from the state was in the first folder. The paperwork clearly stated that she was legally blind.

I wasn't entirely sure what she meant, so I Googled it on my phone and discovered that meant that she could still have some eyesight. Yet, everyone believed she was completely blind.

I closed the web browser on my phone and quickly took a picture of the paperwork. Just as I got the photo, I heard the front door open. I crept out into the upstairs hallway and saw that no one was at the bottom of the stairs, so Meri and I went down as quickly and quietly as we could. Whoever had come in was doing something in the basement, so we slipped out the back door. I'd put the key back in the rock just in case, and there was no time to relock the back door. I just had to hope that no one noticed.

We were about to leave the yard when someone else pulled up in the driveway. Rather than get caught in the backyard, Meri and I hid behind the garden shed until we decided that we could get out without someone seeing us. While we were hiding, I saw some vines peeking out of the back door of the shed that looked like they'd been clumsily hacked or torn off.

My car was parked a couple of blocks over, so while we walked back, I put my headset in and pretended to talk on my phone. The last thing I needed was for someone to spot me talking to Meri.

"I saw some vines sticking out of the back door of the shed," I whispered to Meri. "Are castor beans grown on vines?"

"I don't think they're vines like you'd traditionally think, but I could see how they might look that way once they were cut. What did they look like?"

"Here, I snapped a pic really fast before we left," I said and showed him my screen.

Then, I did another quick Google search for castor bean plant and found that the plants I'd seen were castor bean plants. The shape of the leaves was pretty unmistakable.

"Yeah," Meri said when I showed him the search results. "That definitely looks like the picture you took."

"Those had to be the castor bean plants stolen from Ruby's garden. I saw the ends of some of them and they looked like they'd been hacked off with dull scissors or just torn. We're going straight to the sheriff. We've got her," I said.

We were about halfway to the sheriff's office when Meri told me to just go home. "We can't tell Thorn about this, Brighton. We were breaking and entering when you got the information. None of it is admissible in court, and he might arrest you."

"Fudge," I said. "You're right."

So we went back to Hangman's House instead. A while later, when Meri and I had pretty much given up on finding a way to bust Hattie, the doorbell rang.

Much to my surprise, it was Annika with pizza and beer. "I hope you don't mind me dropping by unannounced, but I come bearing gifts," she said and handed me the pizza box. "Also, I love the new hair. It's so fierce."

My hand went unconsciously to smooth my ponytail. "Thanks, but it wasn't intentional.

It started when I was trying to feel my magic on the ley line."

"Well, that's cool. I've heard that coming into your power can change you physically. At least you didn't get warts. Did your boobs get bigger too? I always hoped mine would get bigger with my practice, but of course, I can't actually use my magic for that. Personal gain and all."

"I think my boobs are the same size," I said and looked down to be sure. "I'll let you know if that changes."

We went into the living room and I set the pizza down on the table. Annika got two beers from the six-pack and then put the rest in the fridge.

"So tell me what's on your mind. I can tell it's something more serious than boobs and hair color," she said before shoving about half the slice of pizza in her mouth.

I downed a huge chug of beer and then blurted out: "I think Hattie killed Harkin, and I think she broke in here and tried to steal my family grimoire."

"Whoa," Annika said before stuffing the other half of the pizza slice in her mouth. "This is really good," she mumbled with her mouth full.

"So someone broke in here and tried to steal the book. They put a spell on me to paralyze me, but Meri ran them off. He smelled lavender and baby powder. It made him sneeze," I rambled. "When I stayed at Hattie's that's exactly how she smelled."

"Okay."

"So I kinda broke into her house, but not really. She had a key in a really fake-looking rock by her back door. Anyway, she's only legally blind. She might not be totally blind, Annika," I said and took a deep breath. "Someone came back while we were in there, so Meri and I had to hide out behind her shed. I found castor bean plants back there. I think they were the ones stolen from Ruby's garden."

"I never really liked Hattie," Annika said. "I don't know what it is, but something about her has always rubbed me the wrong way.

I never said anything, though, because everyone around town thinks she's some sweet, innocent old lady."

"I don't know what to do because Thorn doesn't believe she can see. He thinks she's totally blind too. I got pictures of the paperwork saying she's just legally blind, but I can't turn them in. I was breaking and entering," I said as my shoulders slumped in defeat.

"Let's get another beer," Annika said, and I realized we'd drained the first ones. "Another beer and we'll come up with a plan."

We drank another beer and finished the pizza. When I was about to get up to throw the box away, I saw Annika's eyes light up.

"I've got it," she said and snapped her fingers. "We'll call in an anonymous tip." That was followed by a belch and a giggle fit.

"You know what?" I asked, feeling warm and light from the beer. "That might actually work."

"Here use my phone," she said and handed it to me.

"Shouldn't we go find a payphone or something?"

"I don't think there are any payphones anymore. Don't worry, if you stay on for less than thirty seconds, they can't trace it. I'm sure of it."

"I can't do it. I'm too nervous," I said and handed the phone back to her.

"Fine, I'll do it," she said and dialed the non-emergency number. "Can't call 911 because I think they can definitely trace that," she said as it rang. "Yes, hello, this is Mrs. Cornfield," Annika said in a strange deep voice, and I had to stifle a giggle. "I have a tip for the police. That Hattie Driggs is the one who murdered Professor Max Harkin. She's not really blind, and she's got the murder beans in her garden shed."

Annika quickly hung up the phone and we both burst out laughing. "I can't believe you did that," I said.

"We should have the last beers," she said. "We'll celebrate being the ones who took down a murderer."

Ten minutes later, we were laughing and drinking our last beers when the doorbell rang. "Shh, it might be the FBI here to interview us," I said which sent us into another fit of laughter.

I opened the door and found a very annoyed-looking Thorn staring back at me. "You want to tell me what's going on?"

"What do you mean?" I asked as innocently as I could manage.

"Someone called in an anonymous," and he did the air quote signs for the word anonymous, "tip that Hattie Driggs murdered Max Harkin. Except that it wasn't anonymous because the call came from Annika Skeenbauer's phone. Which my friend at the cell phone company helped me track to this address."

"Oh," I said. "We thought that if we were on the phone for less than thirty seconds, you couldn't trace it."

"Can I come in?" he asked and took off his hat. This visit he happened to be in full uniform.

I stepped back and motioned for him to enter. "Please come in."

Thorn walked in and Annika immediately began to giggle again. She covered her mouth with her hand, and Thorn turned to me with an even deeper scowl etched into his handsome face.

"Frivolous police reports are serious business, you two. I could arrest you," he said sternly.

"But it wasn't frivolous," I protested. "It's the truth, and I have proof."

"What do you mean?" Thorn asked.

I retrieved my phone from the coffee table and showed him the picture of Hattie's form saying she was legally blind. I showed him the picture of the torn castor bean plants too.

"She came after me too," I said. "Please don't forget that."

"I don't think that little old lady broke into your house, Brighton, and I don't even want to know how you got those photos. You need to steer clear of this investigation," he said. "I'm leaving now, and I'm not going to arrest you two this time. Please walk me out."

He turned to leave, and I followed him back out to the porch. "What do you need?" I asked as I closed the front door behind me.

"I'm not sure what to make of this," he said and shocked me by pushing a strand of runaway hair that had come loose from my ponytail away from my face. "It's a little extreme, but maybe it suits you." His eyes were far softer than they'd been when we were inside, but I didn't know what to make of that.

"Is that why you wanted me to come out here? You wanted to discuss my hair?" It came out with a sharper edge than I'd intended.

"No. I wanted to tell you again to stay out of the investigation. If you want to be a part of this town, then you need to at least try to fit in here. The hair is one thing, but it's not going to take long for the rumors to fly that you are accusing a beloved old lady of murder. It's not going to make things easy for you around here."

"But, I…" I started to protest again, but Thorn cut me off.

"I have to go. Please just think about what I've said, and please, please, please," he said and steepled his hands in front of his chest as if in prayer, "don't make me come back here tonight and arrest you and Annika."

He left, and I went back in to find Annika trying to look serious. "I'm sorry," she said. "I really thought the thirty-second thing was true. Good thing he's sweet on you."

"He is not sweet on me," I said.

"Then why didn't we get in more trouble? And why was he making googly eyes at you?" she said with a huff. "He's the town's most eligible bachelor, and it figures he'd like you. Your boobs didn't even get bigger."

And with that, we both burst into another fit of laughter. When we calmed down, I finally remembered the thing about the necklace at the grocery store.

"Oh, oh. I have something I need to tell you," I said. "I saw a woman at the grocery store wearing a necklace that sounded like the one you had stolen. She bent over to pick up her grocery bags, and her shirt collar fell open a bit. I saw it right before she pulled her collar back up."

"Really? Who was it?" Annika asked.

"I don't know, but she was a very tall blonde. Looked like she had a lot of money too. She was leaving at the same time I was, and she drove off in a high-end black Mercedes."

"Oh, I think I know who that might be," she said. "I have to go. Meet me at the archives tomorrow. We're going to enlist Remy to help us with the Hattie situation."

"You shouldn't drive," I said.

"Of course. I would never," Annika said and stood up. "I didn't drive here anyway."

"You shouldn't walk either. It's not safe, and I can't give you a ride."

"Don't worry, I texted Remy to give me a lift home. He's the best cousin in the world, and he's in your driveway waiting."

When my doorbell rang an hour later, I assumed it was either Annika or Thorn. I'd thought that perhaps Annika had forgotten something or Thorn had come back to lecture me more, but I was surprised to find Prue on my porch.

"I'm sorry to just drop in," she said while ringing her hands nervously. "I was upset, so I went for a walk. Somehow, I ended up here. I can leave. I'm sorry."

"No, it's okay. Come in," I said. "Would you like some tea or coffee?"

"Tea would be great," she said. "Thank you."

I went into the kitchen and made us some tea, and when I came back, Prue was sitting on the sofa with Meri curled up in her lap. "He's gorgeous," she said and scratched him between the ears.

"He's special, that's for sure," I said and Meri opened one eye to glare at me. "So what's going on?"

"I feel stupid blubbering to a stranger about this, but something just told me to come here. And when you were in my shop *that* day, I just got a feeling about you. I try to trust my gut. Is that weird?"

"It's okay, Prue. You can talk to me," I said and took a sip of my tea.

"Okay, so my shop is kind of in ruins. People keep returning the chocolates saying they are bitter. I don't know what to do. What's even worse is that the rumor is going around that my chocolates are bitter because I've poisoned them. They think I killed Max, and I guess the whole town thinks I'm trying to wipe them out too." The last part brought tears to her eyes. "Would you try one and tell me if they are bitter? I've tasted them, and I have no idea what they are talking about."

Prue pulled a box of chocolates out of her purse, opened it, and offered the selection to me. For a moment I hesitated because even though I knew she hadn't killed Harkin, I wondered if perhaps she was a crazy woman who was trying to poison the town. Stranger things had happened. Still, I chose a square piece that didn't look like it had any filling and took a small bite. It was quite bitter. I'd had dark chocolate before, but Prue's candy was so unpleasant that I almost had to spit it out.

She saw the look on my face, and the tears pooling in her eyes began to stream down her face. Prue sobbed, and I unconsciously took another bite of the chocolate. That bite was ten times as bitter as the previous bite, and it had a salty aftertaste. I had to run into the kitchen and spit it out.

It was almost as if... "Prue, do you have any kind of... abilities?"

"You mean beyond making candy?"

"Yeah, I mean... I'm not sure how to put this... Like... Maybe spiritual abilities? That might sound crazy, but I have to ask."

"You mean do I have any magic? Am I a witch?"

I nodded my head yes.

"No one knows," Prue said. "Everyone in Coventry thinks I'm a regular human. I'm not from one of the founding families, but I am from a long line of kitchen witches."

"That explains what's happening, Prue. Your emotions are going into your candy. You're upset about the way Harkin treated you, and it's affecting the food you make."

"Oh, wow," she said thoughtfully. "I hadn't thought about that."

"But you should know that you didn't deserve to be treated the way Harkin treated you. He was just a nasty man who hid his true colors from you, and then you got a glimpse of the real man when you got too close. You don't deserve to have your business ruined because of one terrible man."

"Thank you," she said and wiped her tears away with the back of her hand. "Thank you so much, Brighton. I guess my intuition was right to lead me here."

"You're welcome. I need friends in this town, and I'm glad that I can count you as one of them," I said and popped another chocolate in my mouth. It was filled with pecan cream that exploded with rich delicious flavor in my mouth. "And your chocolates are perfect again. That one was delicious."

"Oh, good," she said and smiled. "I'll have a sale to get people back in the door. People love sales, and when they find out that the candy is good again, everything will be okay."

"Glad I could help," I said. "So can I keep these?"

"On the house," Prue said before pulling me into a bear hug.

Chapter Twelve

The next day I got a text shortly before lunch time to meet Remy and Annika at the archives. I got there, and the two of them filled me in on the plan.

"Okay, so Remy and I are going to stage a conversation for Hattie to overhear. We're going to make up a conversation about the extensive collection of Tuttlesmith spell books you just found in Hangman's House. Then we'll all hide at your house and wait for her to break in again."

"You think she'll buy that?" I asked.

"I think she'll be too tempted to not at least try and have a look for herself," Remy said. "If she risked breaking in for that one book, imagine what she'd do if she thought there were even more."

"But what if she's dangerous?"

"Don't worry, Brighton. Remy and I have got your back."

"So when is this going to happen?" I asked.

"Right now. Hattie goes to Dumbledore's for the daily special once a week, and today is her day. We're going to go get a table near her, which we should be able to do since it's early, and I'll call you."

"Wait, that's it? You're going now. Why didn't you just call me or text me and let me know?"

"Because we can't exchange intelligence as important as this over the phone," Annika said with a huff.

"Well, can't I go with you? We can all talk about the books."

"No, that wouldn't work because Remy and I are going to pretend to be completely jealous of your new books. We can't do that with you there. But you could totally go and sit on the other side. That might sell the whole thing even more. People will think we've all had a falling out, and Hattie won't realize we're working together."

"I have to go sit alone?" I asked.

Remy and Annika both nodded their heads yes.

"Fine, but one of you is paying for my pancakes," I said.

"I will," Remy volunteered quickly and then blushed furiously. "I mean, I don't mind."

I waited ten minutes after they left and then departed the archives for Dumbledore's Diner. When I arrived at the diner, I sat on the other side of the restaurant as Remy and Annika shot me fake dirty looks. They'd gotten a table right behind Cassidy and Hattie, so the plan was working. I gave Cassidy a small wave, and she smiled in return.

It would have been hard not to watch Annika and Remy the whole time, so I sat with my back to them. I'd have to find out later if the plan worked, but at least I was getting free pancakes.

Keisha came over to take my order. "Remy said to get you whatever you wanted on him," she said with a smile. "He said I had to keep it a secret from everyone but you, though. I think he's got a bit of a crush. A girl could do worse."

I ordered my usual pancakes but got them with a side of cheesy hash browns instead of bacon. Remy was only paying for my lunch because I'd demanded it, but I couldn't help wondering about what

Keisha had said about a girl doing worse. He seemed sweet and kind, and while Remy wasn't a blond-haired, blue-eyed Adonis like Thorn, he was easy on the eyes. His big brown eyes were rimmed with thick lashes, and he was tall with a lean frame that a lot of women, including me, found attractive. I found myself wondering if Remy blushed when he talked to me because he thought the same thing.

By the time I finished my food, Remy, Annika, Cassidy, and Hattie were all gone. Their tables had been cleaned and new patrons occupied them. I debated going to the archives, but after a lunch spent contemplating whether Remy liked me or not, I didn't think I could face him just yet. I might have turned into a blushing mess, and I wasn't sure if I was ready for that.

At dinnertime, I was thinking about calling Annika because she hadn't called me yet. Just as I was about to dial, my phone rang.

"Sorry," she said. "I was going to call you sooner but Mrs. Kenner came into my store this afternoon. She's a regular customer who also happens to be a tall, rich blonde. I caught her stealing, Brighton. All because you tipped me off. Anyway, Thorn came and arrested her when he looked at the surveillance tapes. I should have installed them sooner, but better late than never, right?"

"Right," I said.

"So sorry for the late call. But I have good news. Hattie definitely overheard my conversation with Remy at the diner. We heard her give Cassidy the night off too, so we think she's going to make her move tonight. What time do you think you'll go to bed?"

"Probably around ten," I said.

"Awesome. Remy and I will see you then. Don't wear slutty pajamas," she said and hung up.

I was going to say that I didn't own any slutty pajamas, but she'd disconnected before I could protest. After making some popcorn, I settled in to watch a movie until bedtime. It wasn't long before I became nervous that Hattie might try to break in before I went to bed.

Can you come over now? I sent the text to Annika.

Be there in ten. She responded.

Eight minutes later, Annika was ringing my doorbell. "Remy's parking the car a couple of streets over," she said. "He'll be here in a few minutes."

After he showed up, we watched the movie with the lights off so no one could see that there were three people in the house. When it was over, we turned out all of the lights and I pretended to go to bed.

Annika and Remy hid in my closet with sleeping bags, and I closed my eyes and faked sleep. I tried to go to sleep for real because I knew Hattie wouldn't come until the middle of the night, but I was too tense to rest. I lay awake for a long time just listening for the sounds of someone breaking into my home.

A few hours later, I must have drifted off. I was awakened by a ruckus coming from the attic library. I don't know why we thought she'd come into the bedroom again, but Hattie had gone straight to the library.

I charged up the narrow steps and found Hattie ransacking the collection of books nearest the back wall. She was wearing a ski mask and purple housecoat, but there was no doubt that it was Hattie.

She tried to whisper the paralyzing spell again, but I already knew that it wouldn't work if I didn't let it. I called for Annika and Remy, but before they could make it up the steps, the attic door raised and shut them out. I could hear them pulling on the chain, but it wouldn't open. I tried in vain to open it from my side, but it was stuck. That spell I didn't know how to counter. Believing I could open the door wasn't opening it.

If it wasn't already clear to me that Hattie was better trained in magic, it became so quickly. Books came flying off the shelves at me without her even having to wave her hands. She did it all with her mind.

"I know why you want the books," I said as I jumped out of the way of a flying tome, "but why did you kill Harkin?"

Another book flew off the shelf and at my head as a broad smile spread across her face. "He thought he could fool me, but he was the fool," she said and cackled. "That Harkin tried to steal from me, and you don't steal from Hattie Driggs."

I dodged the book and knelt down to escape another that barely flew over my head. "What do you mean he stole from you?" I hoped I could distract her and slow down the barrage of books long enough to find a way to escape.

"He paid me in cash, but he thought I was totally blind. So he'd fold the bills up to hide that he was slipping in one-dollar bills when they was 'sposed to be twenties."

"That was pretty stupid considering you have Cassidy working for you. I wonder why he thought he'd get away with it."

Just then, the next book she'd intended to fling at my head fell to the floor with a thump. Hattie put her hands on her hips and cocked one of them out to the side.

"You know what, you're right. I can't..."

She was cut off when Meri jumped out from under a table and tackled her head. I looked under the table and saw a black hole big enough for the cat. Meri had tunnels in the walls.

Hattie let out a screech and grabbed Meri. She flung him across the room and he hit the wall with a sickening thump. Looking at him lying there not moving made fury rise up in me like I'd never felt before.

The rug on the floor in front of me rose up and wrapped around Hattie. It knocked her to the floor and rolled her up so she could barely squirm.

A second later, the attic steps finally released, and I heard Annika and Remy running up the stairs. I rushed to Meri and ran my hand over his still body. A lump rose in my throat, but just before the tears could break free, he opened on eye.

"Is it over yet?" he asked and sat up.

"You're alive. Oh, gosh," I said and pulled him into my arms. "You're still not my cat, but I'm so happy you're alive."

"I can't die because of that Skeenbauer curse, remember," he said as he tried to wriggle free. "This is undignified."

But a moment later, he pressed his furry little forehead against my neck and let me snuggle him for a moment. "I'm going to give you all the smoked salmon you can handle. You're so brave."

"How are we going to afford that?" he said as I let him go.

"Probably with this," Remy said.

He picked up one of the books that Hattie had flung at my head. The inside pages had been hollowed out, and stuff inside were several stacks of hundred-dollar bills.

"Here's another one," Annika said and picked up another book stuffed full of hundreds.

"I'm going to call the sheriff to come deal with her," I said as Remy and Annika looked through the discarded books for more cash. "You guys had better keep this a secret. The last thing I need is the whole town knowing I have a secret library full of cash."

I didn't say anything else because I really liked Annika, but I was more worried about her grandmother finding out about my fortune than the rest of the town.

Chapter Thirteen

Thorn was more than a little sheepish when he arrived a few minutes later. "I'm sorry I underestimated Hattie," he said. "And I'm sorry I didn't listen to you."

"Apology accepted," I said.

"But," and then he had to ruin it, "you are not an investigator and you'd be better off staying out of my way."

"Hey, Thorn," Annika sniped, "I'll have you know that we're excellent investigators. We set this trap to catch Hattie, and we did it."

"Well, that was stupid, reckless, and probably illegal," Thorn said.

"You're just mad that I'm a better investigator that you," I said and instantly regretted it. He'd just gotten under my skin.

"I'm going to take Ms. Driggs into custody now," he said curtly. "I hope the three of you can stay out of trouble for the rest of the night."

When he was gone, I invited Annika and Remy to stay in the guest rooms. I hadn't really done anything with them yet, but it appeared that the house had taken care of that for me.

We were up until almost dawn waiting for the adrenaline to wear off. I began to worry that Hattie would escape Thorn's custody.

"No, she won't be able to get away. Thorn can arrest witches who break the law and hold them because he's under a powerful protection spell cast by the law-abiding witches in Coventry. It gives him the unconscious ability to nullify their harmful magic and arrest the resistors. But he's not a witch and has no idea he's been given that power," Remy said when I expressed my concerns.

"This wasn't exactly the best introduction to our little town, but are you going to stay in Coventry?" Annika asked.

"I was just planning on staying here long enough to fix up the place and sell it, but how could I walk away from my legacy and my potential power?" I said. "Plus, who would leave friends like you guys and Meri?"

Meri purred when I included him and rubbed him between the ears. He was kind of a snarky little beast, but at least he was being nice when I needed him the most.

I was a little worried about how Amelda would react to the news that I had no intention of leaving. More than that, I was concerned about how Thorn was going to take it. The look on his face when he'd left earlier told me he wasn't exactly thrilled with me, and we'd barely gotten along during our interactions. Added to that was the fact that he probably thought I was nuts.

But why did I care? It wasn't like we had to be friends. We just had to find a way to make peace with each other. Plus, it wasn't like I was going to be involved in another murder mystery...

Epilogue

I'd finally drifted off to sleep on the sofa. Despite me offering the guest rooms to Remy and Annika, they were asleep in their sleeping bags on the floor.

The scratching noise had returned, and the hair on the back of my neck stood up. I'd assumed that the incident I'd had before was either a nightmare or Hattie messing with me.

But as my eyes came into focus, I saw the woman in the white gown again. She was scratching on the front door, and then she drifted through it.

I stood up and padded my way quietly to the front door so as not to wake Meri, Remy, and Annika. As I closed the front door behind me, I saw her standing in the front yard, then she drifted across the street to a field on the other side of the road. There was a low fence, but I easily stepped over it.

The area was a small section of forest between my neighborhood and the main part of town. I'd seen it every time I came out of the house, but until then, I'd never given it any thought. As the woman in white disappeared deeper into the trees, I felt compelled to follow her.

Something hard on the ground caught my foot, and I fell down to my knees. When I looked back to see what had tripped me, I found the bottom portion of a gravestone that had broken off some time in the distant past. My eyes scanned the area, and I saw that there were more headstones. Some of them were broken, but others were just obscured by weeds and vines. I'd stumbled into some sort of unmarked cemetery.

The woman in white was gone, but the wind began to pick up. It rose until it was nearly a deafening howl. Black mist began to rise up from the graves, and the smell of roses filled my nostrils. I had to cover my ears because the wind became so loud that it made my head pound.

I turned and ran out of the forest area. I'd thought I was only in the cemetery for a minute or two, but as I climbed the fence and crossed the street, it occurred to me that the sun was breaking the horizon. Somehow, it was morning.

And in my driveway was Thorn's cruiser. He was sitting on my porch.

"What were you doing in there?" he said, looking me over. I must have been a mess with windblown hair and dirt on the knees of my pajamas.

"Thought I saw a dog run in there," I said quickly.

"Are you all right?" he asked, and I saw something that looked like genuine concern and affection on his face. It caught me off guard again when he brushed some of my hair away from my face.

"I'm okay. But I should ask you why you're on my porch at the crack of dawn."

He pressed his lips together in a line for a moment. "That's why I'm here. I wanted to make sure that you're okay."

"Really?"

"Yeah," he said and took a step closer to me. "I don't know what it is about you, Brighton. The hair. Your energy. All of it... It intrigues me in a way I didn't expect."

"Oh," I said and swallowed the nervous lump in my throat.

"Does that bother you?"

"No," I said, but then I got this weird feeling of discomfort.

It was like I was worried that Remy might be watching. And I suddenly didn't know if I cared if Remy was watching or not because why would I care about that? It wasn't like I liked Remy, was it?

All of that was running through my mind as Thorn leaned in. He moved his hand under my chin and tipped my face up. "I want to kiss you," he said, but then he lingered there for what felt like an eternity. When he didn't move the rest of the way in, I bit my bottom lip in anticipation.

I nodded my head yes, because Thorn had successfully drawn my attention completely to him. I wanted him to kiss me too, and I'd figure out the rest later.

A nanosecond before his lips touched mine, his radio squawked, and I jumped back a foot. There was a fight at the tavern.

"I have to go," he said. "Another time?"

"Another time," I confirmed.

But as I went back into the house and saw Remy asleep on my living room floor, I found myself happier than I expected that we'd been interrupted. His eyes opened as I made my way toward the kitchen.

"Coffee?" I whispered.

"Yes, please," he whispered back.

He pulled himself up off the floor and followed me into the kitchen quietly. I put the coffee on and got a couple of cups from the cabinet.

"An interesting night," I said absentmindedly.

"Yeah," he answered. "So what were you doing outside?"

"Oh, that? Well, this house is haunted, and I followed a ghost across the street to a haunted cemetery."

"Really?" He perked up. "I'd heard rumors that there was a secret graveyard in Coventry, but I've never been able to find it. Figures it's across the street from your house."

"I don't really want to go back there alone, but do you want to go check it out when we're done with our coffee?" I asked.

"That would be awesome," he said, and then that endearing blush crept across his cheeks again.

"It's a date."

Made in United States
Troutdale, OR
06/26/2023

10815006R00127